and the
Pantomime

Also by Kaye Umansky

Pongwiffy Back on Track
Pongwiffy A Witch of Dirty Habits
Pongwiffy and the Goblins' Revenge
Pongwiffy and the Spell of the Year
Pongwiffy and the Holiday of Doom
Pongwiffy and the Spellovision Song Contest

Clover Twig and the Incredible Flying Cottage

PONGWIFFY

and the
Pantomime

Kaye Umansky

Illustrated by Nick Price

BLOOMSBURY

LONDON BERLIN NEW YORK

Bloomsbury Publishing, London, Berlin and New York

This edition published in Great Britain in 2009 by Bloomsbury Publishing Plc
36 Soho Square, London, W1D 3QY

First published by Puffin Books 1997

Text copyright © Kaye Umansky 1997
Revised text copyright © Kaye Umansky 2009
Illustrations copyright © Nick Price 2009

The moral rights of the author and illustrator have been asserted

All rights reserved
No part of this publication may be reproduced or
transmitted by any means, electronic, mechanical, photocopying
or otherwise, without the prior permission of the publisher

A CIP catalogue record of this book is available from the British Library

ISBN 978 0 7475 9689 9

FSC
Mixed Sources
Product group from well-managed
forests and other controlled sources
Cert no. SGS - COC - 2061
www.fsc.org
© 1996 Forest Stewardship Council

Typeset by Dorchester Typesetting Group Ltd
Printed in Great Britain by Clays Ltd, St Ives Plc

1 3 5 7 9 10 8 6 4 2

www.bloomsbury.com
www.kayeumansky.com

CHAPTER ONE

A Brilliant Idea

'**N**o!' shouted Grandwitch Sourmuddle, thumping the table with her clenched fist. 'No-no-no-no-NO! We are *not*, positively, absolutely, definitely *not* holding a coffee morning, d'you hear? I hate coffee and I detest mornings. All that sitting around with your little finger stuck out, it's not natural. Never, I say! Never, never, never!'

She gave a final thump, folded her arms and sat back, glaring. There was a short pause.

'I take it that's a no, then, Grandwitch?' asked Witch Greymatter, who was secretary that night.

'Yes,' said Sourmuddle emphatically. 'No. Yes, no, that is.'

 1

Greymatter took up her pencil and scribbled through the last item on the list that lay before her.

'Well, that's that, then,' she said with a little sigh. 'We've been through all the suggestions. Jumblesale – barndance – quiznight – craftfair – sponsoredknit – paintyourbroomstickinafunnywayday – swimminggala – flowershow – coffeemorning.'

There fell another silence.

'It's no good,' said Witch Sludgegooey finally. 'I just can't seem to get excited about any of them.'

It was the usual monthly Coven Meeting in Witchway Hall. Twelve Witches and their assorted Familiars sat around the long table set centre stage. Outside, the chilly winds of autumn prowled around the place, rattling at the windows and whistling through every knothole.

So far, the Meeting hadn't gone well. The main item on the agenda was to think of a way in which they could boost the kitty. Christmas was fast approaching and Coven funds were horribly low. Besides, there's something about that in-between time after Hallowe'en and before the end of December that makes you want to fill it with – well, something.

'Tea-break time, I think,' announced Sourmuddle to general relief. 'I've got brain-ache. How are you doing with those sandwiches, Pongwiffy? We're all starving out here!'

 2

'On my way-hee!' sang a cheerful voice from the backstage kitchen. 'Wow, have I got a feast for you!'

There followed a loud yell, a resounding crash and a lot of tinkling.

There was a short pause, then the thirteenth Witch advanced from stage left. A piece of ham stuck to the sleeve of her disreputable cardigan. Her shoes were wet and steaming. She was holding a china handle – all that remained of the Coven teapot. Perched on her hat was a small, grim-faced hamster. He was attempting to wipe what appeared to be a large dollop of mustard from his front.

'Oops!' said Pongwiffy sheepishly.

There were a lot of tuttings, black looks and mutterings of 'typical'.

'I dropped the tray tripping over Hugo,' explained Pongwiffy. 'Blame him. It's all his fault.'

'It *not*,' snapped the Hamster on the hat.

'Of course it is. How was I supposed to know you were right under my feet? If you weren't such a little squirt, I'd have noticed you, wouldn't I?'

'So I take it there's no sandwiches, then?' interrupted Sourmuddle.

''Fraid not,' confessed Pongwiffy. 'There's a nice piece of ham here, fresh off my cardigan, if anybody would like to . . . No? I'll eat it myself, then.' Which she proceeded to do, with relish.

'Sit down, Pongwiffy, and don't say another word,' ordered Sourmuddle.

The failed sandwich-maker pulled out a chair and sat on it, still chewing.

'Now what?' demanded Witch Macabre. 'How are we supposed tay have a tea break if there's noo tea?'

'We think we should call it a night and go home, don't we, Bag?' said Witch Agglebag, stifling a yawn.

'We certainly do, Ag,' replied her twin, Witch Bagaggle. 'We've got two cauldrons full of hot soup at home, just waiting for us to soak our feet in.'

'Can't go home,' ruled Sourmuddle. 'Not until we've made a decision. Besides, I'm all right. I knew it was Pongwiffy's turn to do the catering, so I've brought my emergency flask. Where is it, Snoop?'

'Right here, Grandwitch,' said the small red Demon at her elbow, producing a bright yellow flask with an air of triumph. Everyone watched enviously as he unscrewed the plastic cup and proceeded to pour. Nobody else had thought to bring one.

'Well, I think it's stupid,' grumbled Macabre. 'Having a tea break when there's noo tea.'

'In that case,' said Sourmuddle, taking a sip, 'we'll just have to make small talk.'

'What's that, then?' enquired Macabre suspiciously.

'It's where we chat pleasantly amongst ourselves. Asking about each other's relations and so on,' explained

Sourmuddle. 'For example, I say –' she put on a high-pitched, unconvincing voice, 'I say, "*Dooo* tell me, Witch Sharkadder, how is your delightful cousin, the famous Dwarf chef Pierre de Gingerbeard, of whom we hear you name-drop so much?" And Sharkadder says, "Very well, thank you, Grandwitch, how kind of you to ask."'

'No, I don't,' said Sharkadder tragically, looking up from applying a fresh coat of bright green lipstick. 'Poor Cousin Pierre. He fell into the pancake mix last week. Got badly battered.'

A heavy silence fell as everybody thought sad thoughts about Sharkadder's unfortunate cousin. Outside, the wind moaned. It was all rather depressing.

'Anybody fancy a game of charades?' suggested Pongwiffy in an attempt to brighten things up a bit.

'No,' said Sourmuddle. 'And I thought I told you to keep quiet.'

'How about a sing-song, then? That'd cheer us all up, wouldn't it?'

'We're not here to be cheerful,' Sourmuddle told her severely. 'We're here to think of a moneymaking idea.'

'What have you come up with so far?' asked Pongwiffy, who had been stuck out in the kitchen all night.

'The usual stuff,' sighed Greymatter. 'Nothing we haven't done a hundred times before. Nobody can face another jumble sale, and a quiz night's no good because the Skeletons held one only last week, and the Zombies are having a barn dance, and Sourmuddle's got this thing about coffee mornings . . .'

'Quite right too,' agreed Pongwiffy. 'We don't want to get bogged down in boring old stuff like that. What we need is something challenging. A new, exciting project that makes use of all our amazing talents. Some sort of Christmas show, perhaps. That'd be fun, wouldn't it?'

At this, Witches and Familiars alike sat up and began to look interested.

'You mean, an opera or something?' asked Greymatter, whose tastes ran towards the highbrow.

'Not an opera,' said Pongwiffy definitely. 'Too posh.'

'Us could do a musical, though!' That was Dead Eye Dudley, Sharkadder's battered tomcat. One of his nine lives had been spent as ship's cat on a pirate brig and as a result he was seriously Into Shanties. 'Us could do a musical an' call it *Cats*!'

IdentiKit and CopiCat, the twins' Siamese Cat Familiars, nodded eagerly. Everybody else laughed like drains.

'Ha!' scoffed Pongwiffy. 'Whoever'd want to go and see a show called *Cats*? Craziest idea I've ever heard.'

'Take no notice, Duddles darling,' said Sharkadder coldly. 'Mummy thinks it's a perfectly sweet idea. You can be the star and sing one of your lovely shanties.'

'No, he can't,' argued Pongwiffy. 'What would he sing

about? Fish heads? His flea problem? Scrabbling around in cat litter? You might as well have a musical called – called *Hamsters*!'

Hugo froze in mid-guffaw.

'And vot wrong viz zat?' he enquired stiffly.

'If it comes to it, what's wrong with *Snakes*?' chipped in Slithering Steve, Bendyshanks's Snake.

'Or *Rats*?' piped up Vernon, Ratsnappy's Rat.

'*Vultures* is a catchy title, don't you think?' suggested Barry, Scrofula's Vulture, not very hopefully.

'Or *Haggis*,' poked in Rory, Macabre's Familiar, who was one.

'*Demons*!' (Sourmuddle's Snoop)

'*Fiends*!' (Sludgegooey's Filth)

'*Owls*!' (Greymatter's Speks)

Gaga's Bats flapped about excitedly, obviously making a bid for attention. The only Familiar who didn't have an opinion was Bonidle's Sloth, who, like his mistress, was fast asleep.

'Order!' commanded Sourmuddle, banging her gavel. 'Order, I say! We're not doing a musical about any of you Familiars and that's final. Your job is to help us Witches, not to go swanning off taking starring roles in musicals.'

'Oh no it isn't!' mumbled the Familiars.

'Oh yes it is!' chorused the Witches.

'I've just had a brilliant idea,' said Pongwiffy.

Nobody heard.

'Oh no it isn't!' argued the Familiars, warming to their theme.

'Oh yes it is!' insisted the Witches.

'*I said I've just had a brilliant idea!*' repeated Pongwiffy, more loudly.

Still nobody heard.

'Oh no it isn't!'

'Oh yes it is!'

'I SAID I'VE HAD A BRILLIANT IDEA!'

This time everybody heard. Excitedly, she leapt on to her chair. She had one of those Looks. One of those flushed, bulgy-eyed Looks that everyone knew so well.

'Oh no it isn't!' she squawked. 'Oh yes it is!' She waved dramatically at a point just left of Agglebag's shoulder. 'It's behind you!'

'What is?' said Agglebag anxiously, turning to look.

'No, no, not *really*. I'm just saying that. What does it remind you of?'

'It reminds me that I must ring for the men in white coats to take you away, Pongwiffy,' said Sourmuddle briskly. 'Get down before I lose my temper.'

'Not until you've heard my brilliant idea for the Christmas show,' insisted Pongwiffy.

'Which is?'

'Hold on to your hats, girls,' crowed Pongwiffy, and struck a pose. 'We . . .' She paused for dramatic effect. '*We are going to put on a pantomime!*'

CHAPTER TWO

Which One?

'A pantomime, eh?' mused Sourmuddle. 'I went to one of those once, when I was a slip of a girl. It was all about a poor young woman who did a lot of housework, and a posh fairy in a blue net frock turned up and gave her some grass boots and sent her off to play ball in some sort of converted vegetable. I was sick on ice cream at the interval, I recall. Ah me! Happy days.'

'That was *Cinderella*,' nodded Pongwiffy. 'Although I don't think you've got the plot quite right, Sourmuddle. It was glass slippers, not grass boots.'

'Could be,' agreed Sourmuddle. 'My memory's not what it was. I was definitely sick, though.'

'I don't think it should be *Cinderella*,' said Sharkadder excitedly. 'I vote we do *Dick Whittington*. And I can play the title role, because I've got the right sort of legs for Principal Boy. And Dudley can be my faithful cat.'

'Nonsense,' argued Ratsnappy. 'It's obvious we should do *The Pied Piper*, because I can play the recorder. You said we should make use of our amazing talents, Pongwiffy. And Vernon can be chief rat, can't you, Vernon? And we can use some of your relations as extras.'

Vernon looked excited.

'I think you'll find all the rats get drowned in that story,' remarked Greymatter.

Vernon stopped looking excited and became anxious instead.

'Who'll write it, though?' enquired Bendyshanks. 'I mean, we can't just make it up as we go along. There has to be a proper script and everything.'

'Oh, no problem,' said Pongwiffy rashly. She was much too carried away with her idea to let anything stand in her path. 'I'll write it. It'll probably only take me an evening. I've always fancied myself as a playwright. I'll direct it too. I'll do everything. All we need to do is decide which one. We'll use the little-pieces-of-paper method. Everyone must write down the character she wants to play and we'll see which

11

pantomime crops up most often. Agreed?'

Everyone agreed.

'I'll do the honours, then,' said Sourmuddle, and twiddled her fingers. Instantly, twelve stubby pencils and little scraps of paper materialised on the table before the Witches. Sourmuddle herself had a quill pen and a smart silver inkpot and a large piece of parchment with her name and address prominently displayed at the top, but nobody said anything. She was Grandwitch. She could do what she liked.

'Wazapnin'?' muttered Bonidle, awaking from a deep sleep and finding herself required to do something. 'Is it mornin'?'

'We're putting on a pantomime,' explained Pongwiffy. 'Everyone has to write down who they want to be. If I was you, I'd go for something undemanding, Bonidle. Like a fallen log. Right, off you go.'

There was a bit of excited whispering and the sound of busily scratching pencils.

When everyone had finished, Pongwiffy passed her hat along and they all solemnly dropped their papers in. Sourmuddle made a big thing about rolling up her parchment and tying it with red ribbon before placing it with the others.

'Right,' said Pongwiffy. 'Let's see what we've got.'

Everyone waited with bated breath while she began to unfold the scraps of paper.

'The twins want to be the Babes in the Wood,' she announced. Agglebag and Bagaggle nudged each other and giggled. 'Well, that's all right, I suppose. Sharky's sticking with Dick Whittington. Sludgegooey's written . . . *Snow White*?'

'That's me,' said Sludgegooey eagerly. 'I've always thought of myself as a Snow White sort of person.'

Everyone's jaws dropped in disbelief.

'I'd wash,' she added defensively.

'Hmm,' said Pongwiffy, unpersuaded. She turned to the next piece. 'Bonidle's put Sleeping Beauty. No problem there, she can do it with her eyes closed. Bendyshanks wants to be . . . *Cleopatra*?'

'Oh, I do, I do!' cried Bendyshanks, all aglow with enthusiasm. 'I've always wanted to play her. I did a course on belly dancing once. And Steve can be my poisonous asp. Oh, say I can, Pongwiffy! It's the answer to a dream!'

'Oh dear,' groaned Pongwiffy. 'This is going to be harder than I thought. Ratsnappy's sticking with the Pied Piper, and Scrofula's gone for – wait for it – Rapunzel.'

The assembled company rocked with mirth and tapped their foreheads pityingly.

'So?' said Scrofula, who had what can only be described as Problem Hair. 'What's so funny? You said we can be whoever we like.'

13

But Pongwiffy had moved on to the next one and was holding her head in despair.

'What's this say, Macabre? *Lady Macbeth*?'

'Aye,' said Macabre definitely.

'That's not a pantomime character,' objected Bendyshanks.

'Neither's Cleopatra,' snapped Macabre.

'She can dance, though,' shot back the would-be Queen of the Nile. 'I bet Lady Macbeth never went on a belly-dancing course.'

'She wouldnae want to,' scoffed Macabre. 'None o' that sissy stuff up in Scotland.'

Pongwiffy sighed, and turned to the three remaining suggestions. Greymatter had, for some reason, plumped for Sherlock Holmes. Sourmuddle's childhood experience had apparently left her with a deep-seated desire to be a posh fairy in a blue frock. Last of all was Gaga's piece of paper, on which was written, in wildly enthusiastic writing,

PANTOMIME HORSE –
BACK END PREFERRED!!!!

'Well,' said Pongwiffy despairingly. 'This is ridiculous. There's not even two characters from the same story. Some of you have got to change.'

'Not me,' said Sourmuddle stoutly. 'I'm leader of

this Coven. If I can't be a fairy, I don't want to be in it.'

'But it's impossible,' argued Pongwiffy. 'How do you come up with a storyline that has to include three princesses, an Egyptian dancing queen, a posh fairy, Lady Macbeth, a couple of lost babies, a rat exterminator, Dick Whittington, a fictional detective and a pantomime horse's bum?'

'Well, that's your problem, Pongwiffy,' said Sourmuddle tartly. 'You said you could write the script in an evening, I seem to remember.'

'Well, yes, but –'

'There you are, then. It'll be a nice challenge for you. I suggest you take it home and work on it.'

And that is exactly what Pongwiffy did.

CHAPTER THREE

The Goblins' Invitation

West of Witchway Wood, on the foothills of the Lower Misty Mountains, lies an area of outstanding natural unsightliness, known as Goblin Territory. It is a bleak, windblown place, full of craggy rocks and drippy caves. Nothing grows there, apart from scrubby gorse bushes, the odd twisted tree and unpleasant plants of the stinging variety. You would have to be really stupid to live in Goblin Territory.

Being stupid was something that came easily to the Gaggle of Goblins who lived there in the biggest, dampest, drippiest cave of them all: Plugugly, Stinkwart, Hog, Slopbucket, Lardo, Eyesore and

 16

Sproggit. Seven daft Goblins with six brain cells between them.

Right now, they had just woken up and were thinking about breakfast. Not doing anything about it, you understand, because there wasn't any. Just thinking about it.

'I wish we 'ad sausages,' sighed Stinkwart as they sat in a gloomy circle, staring at the empty frying pan. 'Six fat bangers sizzlin' in a pan. Lovely.'

'There's seven of us,' Slopbucket reminded him. 'I fink,' he added doubtfully. (Goblins are not good at counting. They get confused after two.)

'I know *that*,' said Stinkwart pityingly. 'Fink I'm stupid? I said six 'cos then I can 'ave two, see?'

The Goblins thought about this for a while. There seemed something a bit wrong with Stinkwart's maths, but nobody was sure enough to say so.

'How come Stinkwart gets two?' remarked Eyesore after a bit. 'Two's more than one, innit? How come he gets two sausages and the rest of us only gets one? Huh? Huh?'

'Because I thought of 'em!' cried Stinkwart triumphantly. 'I thought of 'em, so I gets the most. Right?'

'I'll fight you for the extra one,' challenged Slopbucket, flexing his muscles. Everyone cheered up. An early morning punch-up over non-existent sausages wasn't quite as good as eating breakfast, but it

 17

was a way of filling in the time.

The fight, however, never got off the ground, because just at that moment, there came a knock on the front boulder. Everyone looked startled. Visitors were rare, particularly at this hour of the morning.

'Go on, Plug,' chorused six voices. 'See who it is.'

Plugugly reached for the saucepan he habitually wore on his round, bald head. He was the official doorkeeper and he liked to look properly dressed. He stumped to the boulder, rolled it a tiny way to one side and spoke through the crack.

'Yes?' he said. 'Whatcha want?'

'It is the post,' a gravelly voice informed him. 'I is your Post Troll. I has brung you A Letter.'

'Derrr – a what?' said Plugugly.

'A Letter,' repeated the voice, adding helpfully, 'It is a paper fing wiv a stamp on.'

'Cor,' said Plugugly, quite overwhelmed. The Goblins had never had A Letter before.

There was a crackling noise and a square white envelope slid through the gap and fell with a plop at his feet. Nervously, Plugugly stooped and picked it up. The rest of the Goblins shuffled up and peered over his shoulder. It was addressed to:

The Goblins, The Cave
Goblin Territory, Lower Misty Mountains

 18

* * *

To the Goblins, who couldn't read, it just looked like squiggly black marks.

'Better open it, I suppose,' remarked Eyesore doubtfully. 'Go on, Plug.'

Fingers trembling, Plugugly tore it open. It contained a single card covered with yet more incomprehensible squiggles. The Goblins examined it wonderingly.

'Wot's it say?' asked Sproggit.

'Dunno,' confessed Plugugly. 'Anyone got any idears?'

The card was passed around for inspection.

'Thass an H, innit?' said Hog doubtfully, pointing at a G. But that wasn't much help.

'Wot we gonna do?' wailed Lardo. 'We got A Letter an' we can't read it. Wot we gonna do?'

They stared wildly at each other, biting their knuckles and wringing their hands with frustration.

'I know!' cried Plugugly suddenly. 'We'll get de postie to read it to us!'

Everyone cheered and clapped him on the back. Plugugly glowed. He hadn't had many good ideas lately. Perhaps this was the start of a whole new Good Idears era.

The Post Troll was stomping down the slope, merrily whistling a little ditty entitled 'Post Troll Pete

19

and His Oversized Feet'. He was surprised to hear wild shouts, then find himself suddenly surrounded.

'Read dat,' instructed the Goblin with the saucepan on his head, thrusting out the card.

'What about that magic lickle word?' said the Post Troll, wagging a reproving finger.

The Goblins looked blank.

'You know,' prompted the Post Troll. 'What has you got to say? When you is wanting a favour?'

'Or else?' suggested Slopbucket doubtfully.

'I is referrin' to "please",' the Post Troll told him severely. 'Read that *please*.'

'We can't,' explained Eyesore sadly.

'So you read it,' ordered Plugugly.

The Post Troll gave up. He snatched the card and read: '"The Great Gobbo invites you to a Grand Christmas Eve Fancy Dress Ball at Gobbo Towers. A prize will be awarded for the best costume." There. *Now* what do you say?'

More blank faces.

'T'ank you!' shouted the Post Troll. 'T'ank you!'

'Dat's all right,' said Plugugly. 'Any time.'

Shaking his head in despair, the Post Troll thrust the card back at Plugugly, shouldered his bag and stomped off down the hill.

'Cor,' said Plugugly, sounding quite choked. 'We got an invitation. To a ball.'

They could hardly take it in. The Great Gobbo, chief of all the Goblin tribes, wanted them – *them* – at his ball! What an honour.

'I've always wanted to visit that there Gobbo Towers,' said Lardo wonderingly. 'It's dead swanky. My old mum knew someone what worked up there. There's somethin' called A Hinside Toilet.'

'Nah!' breathed Hog, clutching at his heart. 'That's what you call sophicist ... sophitis ... sosiph ... posh.'

'An' there's a proper table with legs wot you eat off.'

'Imagine eatin' off table legs,' gasped Slopbucket, terribly impressed, as anyone would be who was used to eating off the floor.

'An' the Great Gobbo sits on a whackin' great throne,' continued Lardo. 'An' all these beautiful She-Goblins in pink bikinis feeds him grapes.'

'Oo-er,' gulped his audience, their eyes coming over all glazed at the thought of the She-Goblins in their pink bikinis. Young Sproggit was so overcome he had to go and sit down under a tree.

'What's fancy dress when it's at 'ome?' Eyesore wanted to know.

'I know!' squeaked Hog, jumping around with his arm in the air. 'It's where you dresses up fancy. You has to go lookin' like someone else, see.'

'Well, dat's easy,' said Plugugly, relieved. 'We'll swap

clothes an' go as each udder.'

'Erm – no, I don't fink that'll do,' said Hog. 'Iss gotta be someone special. Like a Spanish lady. Or a goriller. Iss gotta be a proper costume, see?'

'Sounds tricky,' commented Lardo, shaking his head. 'Proper costumes don't grow on trees.'

Seven anxious pairs of eyes roamed over the few scrubby trees growing on the slope. Nope. No costumes there.

'We'll fink about de costumes,' decided Plugugly. 'We'll 'ave a long, hard fink. We ain't lettin' costumes stop us from goin' to de ball. We just 'ave to use our 'eads. Right?'

The Goblins looked at each other doubtfully.

'I 'ad my 'ead examined once,' remarked Lardo. 'They couldn't find nuffin'.'

And, brows furrowed in deep concentration, they made their way back up to the cave in order to begin the unaccustomed process of thinking.

CHAPTER FOUR

The Script

'I think I've got writer's block,' announced Pongwiffy. She was wading to and fro in a sea of inky puddles and screwed-up pieces of paper in Number One, Dump Edge, which is the hovel where she lives. Obviously, things were not going well on the creative front.

'Vot ze problem?' asked Hugo, who was sitting in a teacup, filling in *The Daily Miracle* crossword puzzle.

'What's the *problem*?' cried the demented playwright, clutching her head with ink-stained fingers. 'I'll tell you the problem. I've got a cast of thousands which I've somehow got to fit into a storyline. I've got to think of jolly songs and some dances and a happy ending. And there's got to be a funny bit with a horse and a bit where everyone goes, "He's behind you!" And everything has to be in rhyming couplets – and that's hard, I might tell you.'

Hugo put down the paper with a little sigh.

'Vot you done so far?'

'Not much,' admitted Pongwiffy. 'Right now I'm trying to come up with a plot and a snappy title. The one I've thought of sounds a bit long.'

'Try me.'

Pongwiffy snatched up a piece of paper and read: '*Sherlock Holmes Solves the Mysterious Case of the Missing Babes in the Wood Who are Spotted by Three Princesses After They Have Been Cruelly Left There by Lady Macbeth Riding Half a Pantomime Horse and They Have a Dream About Cleopatra But are Rescued by the Pied Piper and Dick Whittington and They Get Three Wishes from a Fairy and Live Happily Ever After.*'

'Is good plot,' nodded Hugo encouragingly. 'Plenty of action.'

'That's not the plot. That's the title. Oh dear! I knew it was too long.'

'Don't vorry about ze title,' advised Hugo. 'Script first. Title later.'

'I know, I know. But that's easier said than done. These rhyming couplets are very tricky, you know. I've had a go at Sherlock Holmes's opening speech, but I'm stuck.'

'Read me vot you done.'

Pongwiffy fished about and came up with another piece of paper.

'Ahem. "*Enter Sherlock Holmes.*"'

There was a pause.

'Go on,' said Hugo.

'That's it.'

'Zat's *it*? But 'e not say nussink!'

'I know. I told you I was having trouble with his opening speech.'

'Vell,' said Hugo, shaking his head. 'Zat no good. Zis Sherlock, 'e important character. 'E got to 'ave lines to say. 'E got to say sumsink like –' he scratched his head, 'sumsink like, "*I Sherlock 'Olmes. 'Ow do you do? I searchink for a vital clue.*"'

'What?' hissed Pongwiffy, electrified. 'What did you just say, Hugo?'

Hugo looked surprised, gave a little shrug, then repeated it.

'I Sherlock 'Olmes. 'Ow do you do?
I searchink for a vital clue.'

'But it's brilliant!' cried Pongwiffy, casting about for another sheet of paper. 'Hang on, let me write it down!'

Ink sprayed everywhere as she scribbled madly.

'Right. Got it. What might he say next, do you think?'

Hugo pondered briefly, then said:

> *'Ze Babes are missink in ze vood.*
> *No news of zem. Zis is not good.*
> *I' ave to solve zis mystery*
> *Or zose poor Babes is 'istory.'*

'Hugo! But this is sheer poetry! I never knew you had it in you!'

Pongwiffy's pen fairly flew as she committed the immortal lines to paper.

'Go on!' she begged. 'What happens next?'

'Vell . . .' said Hugo slowly, 'vell, zen zis Sherlock, 'e go off to ze vood to look for ze Babes. And 'oo should 'e meet but Snow Vhite and 'er friends Rapunzel and Sleepink Beauty, dancink gracefully round a tree.'

'Of course! That gets a dance in! Hang on, I must make a note to book the Witchway Rhythm Boys. Right, go on! What do they say?'

Hugo vaulted from the cup, twirled an imaginary skirt, batted his eyelashes and declaimed:

> *'I am Snow Vhite, as you can see.*
> *Zose are my good friends 'ere viz me.*
> *Ve laugh an' play an' 'ave such fun,*
> *And zen ve lie down in ze sun.'*

'Fun! Sun! Incredible!' marvelled Pongwiffy. 'Go on. What does Scrofula say?'

With absolutely no hesitation, Hugo replied:

> *'I am Rapunzel viz long hair*
> *And Sleepink Beauty's over zere.'*

'Amazing! Fantastic! How do you think of it?'

'I dunno,' said Hugo with a modest little shrug. 'It just come, you know?'

'Well, I never!' crowed Pongwiffy, rocking to and fro. 'What talent! And I never even knew. Oh, this is too good to be true!'

Just then there was a knock on the door.

'Cooooeeee! Pong! It's me!' came a voice.

'Botheration! It's Sharky. And just as the panto was beginning to take shape. Go and put your feet up, Hugo, you little genius. Rest your brains for a bit. We'll carry on the minute I get rid of her.'

She scuttled to the door and flung it open.

'Yes? What is it, Sharky? I'm rather busy at the moment. Writing the panto, you know.'

'Oh? Really?' said Sharkadder, peering curiously at the heaps of crumpled paper. 'Well, I won't stop long. It's very cold out here. I don't suppose . . . ?'

She looked hopefully past Pongwiffy in the direction of the kettle.

'No,' said Pongwiffy. 'Not a chance.'

'Oh, well. I'll be off, then. Don't want to interrupt the creative flow. Is it – er – coming along all right?'

'Oh, fine, fine,' declared Pongwiffy. 'I'm getting on like a hovel on fire. It's fairly flowing out of me. Should have it all wrapped up in no time.'

'Well, I never,' breathed Sharkadder, terribly impressed. 'I never knew you were a writer, Pong. It just goes to show. You can be friends with someone for years and not discover all their hidden talents.'

'Amazing, isn't it?' said Pongwiffy with a light little laugh.

'*Ahem!*'

From behind there came the distinct sound of a Hamster's warning cough.

'Have you – er – got to Dick Whittington's bit yet, by any chance?' enquired Sharkadder, trying to sound casual. 'Not that I'm *that* interested, ha ha, it's just that I was wondering if I've got a lot of lines to say. By any chance.'

'You haven't entered yet. You have to be patient. I've got loads of other stuff to fit in first. This is a team effort, Sharkadder. We don't want any prima donnas.'

'Oh. Yes, of course. I quite understand that,' said Sharkadder humbly. 'I'll let you get on, then, shall I?'

She turned and respectfully began to tiptoe away. Then she paused.

'Er – just one thing. I don't have to *kiss* anybody, do I?'

Pongwiffy glanced back at Hugo, who shrugged.

'I don't know yet,' said Pongwiffy furtively. 'Haven't quite decided. If it's in the script, you'll have to. That's show business.'

'Well, I'm not kissing Sludgegooey or any of that lot,' declared Sharkadder firmly. 'Even if I am Principal Boy. I do have some pride. If there's any princess-kissing to be done, you'll need a Prince Charming.'

'Excuse me,' interrupted Pongwiffy sternly. 'Who's writing this panto?'

'Why – you, of course, Pong.'

'Correct,' said Pongwiffy. 'Me. With, perhaps, a bit of help from Hugo. And I don't need to be told how it should be done. Anyway, we don't have a Prince Charming. Nobody wanted to be him.'

'Well, you could always import one. And I've got just the person.'

'Who?' asked Pongwiffy.

Sharkadder told her.

'Don't make me laugh,' said Pongwiffy.

'I'm not. I can't think of anyone else, can you?'

Pongwiffy couldn't. There was a distinct lack of

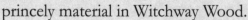

princely material in Witchway Wood.

'That's settled, then,' said Sharkadder gaily. 'We'll go and tell him the good news this afternoon.'

'Well – all right,' sighed Pongwiffy reluctantly, adding, 'Now, if you don't mind, Sharky, I'd like to get back to my script. I feel a couplet coming on.'

And she shut the door.

'There's got to be a Prince Charming, mind,' Sharkadder's voice called faintly. 'It's traditional.'

'She right, Mistress,' said Hugo. 'Zere has. It is.'

'Hmm. All right, we'll stick him in at the end, just before the happy ending. Right, come on then, polish your brains up, Hugo. Let's get this script on the road!'

CHAPTER FIVE

Prince Ronald

Sharkadder's nephew, who was rather grandly known as Ronald the Magnificent (but only to himself), was in his attic room at the Wizards' Clubhouse. Well, actually, it wasn't so much a room. More a cupboard, really.

The allocation of rooms at the Clubhouse was based on the time-honoured Beard System. The Wizard with the longest beard got the big, posh room with the decent rug and the potted plant. The second longest beard was awarded the second poshest (slightly smaller rug, slightly deader plant) – right down to Ronald, who had no beard at all and therefore got the attic with no rug, no plant and everyone else's discarded furniture. Sadly, this didn't include a chair. Ronald spent all his time standing up or lying down, with very little in between.

Right now, he was bent over his desk, which was awash with ancient books, scraps of paper covered in scribbly notes and a host of little jars and bottles filled with mysterious substances. Rising from the clutter was a Bunsen burner, currently set at a low flame under a copper pot. The official name for this pot, as any Wizard will tell you, is a crucible. Ronald's crucible contained a simmering, milky-white substance which was giving off thin wreaths of ghostly white smoke.

It was very clear that some sort of Wizardly experiment was taking place!

In fact, for the last few weeks, Ronald had been secretly working on an exciting, new, mould-breaking formula for an Extra Strong Invisibility Serum. If his calculations were right, a small sprinkle of this wonderful new serum would bring on a state of instant and complete vanishment. There was nothing like it on the market, unless you counted Invisibility Pills (unreliable with a terrible taste) or old-fashioned Cloaks of Invisibility (a shocking nuisance because they were never to be found and always needed dry-cleaning).

The idea had come to him in an inspired flash one day, when he was eating a packet of Polos. If he could just isolate the holes and, using his amazing Wizardly skills, combine them scientifically with a bit of this and a bit of that, and maybe just a touch of the other . . .

Weeks of highly secret research had followed. Long, lonely hours spent huddled over his candle, working out difficult times tables and doing complicated things with a compass. Much poring over the pages of ancient tomes. Much tramping about at dawn in soggy countryside, tracking down various rare plants and herbs. Much eating of Polos.

Still. It was worth it. If the serum worked, he would be the toast of the town in Wizardly circles. He might be asked to write an article about it for *The Wizard's Weekly*. Why, he'd be famous! People might even stop teasing him. People might say things like, 'Say, you've got to hand it to young Ronald, he's really come up with the goods this time. Someone should get him a chair, don't you think?'

And if they didn't, well, see if he cared. He would just bottle the serum up, sell it for a vast profit – and use the money to buy *himself* a chair. A big, flash one. With a cushion. Ha!

Carefully, he measured out half a teaspoon of powder from a little jar labelled 'Dried Scotch Mist' and added it to the bubbling mixture in the crucible. He followed this with a pinch of Essence of Fog and three drops from a small phial containing a black, slippery substance which was, apparently, Extract of

Shadow. There was a series of small explosions as the new substances got to know each other. Then the mixture settled down and simmered away happily. Ronald let out a relieved breath. So far, so good. Now all that remained was to add the final vital ingredient – a handful of Fresh Snow.

Gleefully, he reached for the stoppered flask. Then: 'Blast!' shouted Ronald. 'Blast, bother and blow!'

The flask was empty, apart from a small amount of brackish-looking water. That was the trouble with snow. It had a very short sell-by date. Now he'd have to wait until the next snowfall – whenever that might be – then go out and collect some more. What a disaster!

To add to his troubles, there came the sound of footsteps climbing the stairs. Ronald gave a guilty start, turned off the Bunsen burner, grabbed up the crucible (burning his fingers in the process) and hastily tipped the milky-white stuff down the cracked sink in the corner. He then scooped everything – Bunsen burner, crucible, books, papers, jars, the lot – into a cardboard box, which he kicked under the bed. Finally, he ran around the room, flapping at the air to dispel the white mist and the telltale smell.

The reason for his panic was the small notice that was displayed on his wall. It read:

STRICTLY NO MAGICAL EXPERIMENTS
IN THE BEDROOMS!

It was a sensible rule. In the past, Wizardly research carried out in bedrooms had proved a major fire risk. Alone and unaided, Fred the Flameraiser had burned down the entire Clubhouse at least three times. Of course, with oodles of Magic at their disposal, it didn't take the Wizards long to rebuild it. Nevertheless, it was a terrible nuisance, and nobody could ever agree on the exact shade of wallpaper. In the end, it had been decided that all Magical experiments must be conducted in the special fireproof laboratory which was located in the basement.

The trouble was, the lab was a very public place. Your fellow Wizards tended to wander in, peer over your shoulder, enquire what you were working on, sneer a bit, then sneak off and pinch your idea.

Ronald didn't want anyone to know what he was working on. Not yet. Not until he'd cracked it.

There came a thunderous knocking at the door.

'Just a minute,' called Ronald, snatching up a can of *Reeka Reeka Roses* air-freshener and spraying it around.

Hastily, he threw himself down on his bed and looked casual. Only just in time. The door opened and a head, topped with a tangled green beehive hairdo, peered around it. It was Brenda, the Zombie receptionist.

'You got visitors,' announced Brenda, through a mouthful of bubblegum. 'I told 'em they ain't supposed to come outside of visitin' hours, but –'

'Out of the way, young woman!' interrupted a crisp voice that Ronald recognised with a sinking heart. 'We're here on Witch business!'

The door was flung open and Ronald's visitors stamped in.

'Oh,' said Ronald, rising from his bed with little enthusiasm. 'It's you, Aunt Sharkadder.'

'Good afternoon, Ronald, dear. Pong and I thought we'd pay you a surprise visit. Say hello to Ronald, Pongwiffy.'

Pongwiffy and Ronald curled their lips at each other in mutual dislike.

'So! This is your room, is it?' cried Sharkadder gaily. 'Well, well, well. It's got a funny smell, hasn't it? Like cheap air-freshener with an underlying whiff of cooked marsh gas.'

'That's his aftershave,' said Pongwiffy.

'I hardly think you're in a position to comment on horrible smells, Pongwiffy,' said Ronald with a sniff.

'Actually, I consider myself a bit of an expert,' said Pongwiffy, who did. 'And if you really want to know what I think,' she added, 'I think Ronald's been cooking up a bit of Magic on the sly. Right here, in the shoebox he calls his bedroom.'

'No, I haven't,' lied Ronald, going red.

'Yes, well, I must say I expected something a bit grander,' remarked Sharkadder. 'After everything you've told me, Ronald, I rather had the impression that you Wizards lived in style. Well, come on, then. Haven't you got a kiss for your aunty?'

There came a snigger from the doorway. Ronald went pink. It wasn't done to admit you had a Witch aunty. Particularly one who kissed you.

'All right, Brenda, I won't keep you,' he said uncomfortably. 'Thanks awfully for bringing them up and everything. Er – you won't forget about that chair I asked for, will you? Super earrings, by the way.'

Brenda popped a rude bubble and withdrew. Sharkadder clutched Ronald in a tight embrace and planted a bright green lipsticky kiss on his forehead.

'There!' she said. 'That's because I haven't seen you for ages. How come you never visit me for tea any more, you bad boy?'

'Actually, you haven't invited me,' Ronald pointed out, struggling from her grasp.

'Oh, poo! You're more than welcome any time you like. Day or night, the kettle's always on for my favourite nephew. Haven't I always said that, Pong?'

Pongwiffy was wandering around Ronald's room, fiddling with things. She pulled the handle off his wardrobe. She tried out his bed and broke a spring.

 38

She opened his diary, ran her eyes down a page and sneered.

'You put that down, Pongwiffy,' said Ronald. 'Tell her, Aunty. She's touching my things.'

'Just having a look,' said Pongwiffy. 'Professional interest, you understand. What's this?' She turned a page and read aloud: ' "*1 September: Got up . . . Hung about . . . Had a nurly nite . . . Luked for a char . . . Didunt find one. 2 September: Got up . . . Sossijuss for super . . . Had another nurly nite . . . Still no char.*" Badness me, Ronald, what an exciting life you do lead. What are all these Nurly Nites of which you speak? And what's all this about a char?'

'Stop it! You can't read that – it's private!' Ronald protested and made a leap.

Pongwiffy evaded him and gleefully continued turning pages. 'Aha! Here's something interesting. "*Werked in bedroom on new seecret formuler.*" I knew it! So where's all the stuff? Is that what's in that big cardboard box I see poking out from under your bed?'

'Put it down!' howled Ronald. 'You've got no right to read people's diaries.'

'Oh, all right, keep your hair on. Just thought you might like a few writing tips.'

Pongwiffy threw the diary over her shoulder. Ronald caught it and thrust it deep into his robe.

'Ha!' he scoffed. 'Since when do you know anything

about writing, Pongwiffy?'

'Since I became a playwright, *actually*,' said Pongwiffy with a smug air.

'A playwright? You? Don't make me laugh.'

'I am so. Aren't I, Sharky?'

'Well, yes. As a matter of fact, Ronald, that's why we're here. We've come to offer you a wonderful opportunity. It's a tremendous honour and you're a very lucky young man.'

'Oh, really?' groaned Ronald. He was getting a bad feeling. 'What's that, then, Aunty?'

'You,' announced Sharkadder, 'are going to be Prince Charming in the lovely pantomime that Pongwiffy's writing. Won't that be fun?'

Ronald suddenly came over all weak. His legs gave way and he collapsed on to his bed with a little moan.

'Why?' he managed to choke out. 'Why me?'

'Because there's nobody else,' said Pongwiffy bluntly. 'I didn't really want you, but Hugo says we have to have a prince. To kiss all the princesses.'

'*All* the princesses?' repeated Ronald faintly. 'How many would that be?'

'Three,' said Pongwiffy gleefully. 'Snow White, Rapunzel and Sleeping Beauty. Played by Sludgegooey, Scrofula and Bonidle.'

It was all too much. Ronald rallied.

'No!' he cried. 'I won't do it! I won't!'

'I beg your pardon, Ronald?' purred Sharkadder in a voice like razor blades cutting through silk. 'Did I hear you say you won't?'

'That's right. I'm sorry, Aunty, but I'm a serious Wizard. I'm working on a new project. I can't spare the time.'

'Oh dear. That *is* a pity, isn't it, Pong?'

'It certainly is,' agreed Pongwiffy sadly. 'I guess there's nothing else for it. We'll just have to report him. We'll just have to go down right now and announce that he's been breaking the rules and working on a silly old secret formula in his room. Come on, Sharky. We'll take the evidence with us.'

Purposefully, they moved towards the bed.

'Wait!' cried Ronald.

They paused.

'Yes?' said Sharkadder. 'Is there something you wanted, Ronald?'

'When's the first rehearsal?' said Ronald brokenly.

CHAPTER SIX

The Read-Through

The first rehearsal took place in Witchway Hall. A large circle of chairs had been placed on the stage. Everyone was present, with the exception of the eagerly awaited playwright and her assistant. Ronald was there too, maintaining a stiff air of aloofness and standing apart from the rest of them. This was for the following reasons:

1. It showed he didn't want to be there.
2. No chair. Again.

There was an air of expectancy and great excitement. It was common knowledge that Pongwiffy had finished writing the script. She and Hugo had been shut up in Number One, Dump Edge for days, refusing to answer the door except for important deliveries of ink, paper and takeaway pizzas with extra skunk topping. Various would-be thespians had come knocking to see how their parts were coming along, but to no avail. Gaga's Bats had been sent to spy through the window and had reported scenes of great industry, with candles burning at both ends and a steadily growing pile of manuscript.

Then, that very morning, the hovel door had burst open and the pair of them had staggered out into the fresh air, spraying each other with fizzy demonade and thumping each other's backs in celebratory fashion. When questioned, however, they had refused to give away a thing.

'Wait until this evening,' Pongwiffy had said mysteriously. 'All will be revealed then.'

And now it *was* this evening and the tension was wound up to breaking point. There were a lot of flushed faces, damp palms and peals of high, nervous laughter. People kept saying that, of course, they didn't *mind* if they only got a small part, oh dear me no. But they didn't mean it. Barry the Vulture was so flustered by it all that he had gone off somewhere to be quietly sick. Gaga was in the last stages of complete hysteria and kept rushing off to hang from the curtains.

 43

Only Sourmuddle looked confident. As Grandwitch, she could be sure of a decent part – or, as she told Snoop, she'd want to know the reason why.

Just as the excitement reached fever pitch, the long-awaited writing team arrived. Pongwiffy was clutching a fat sheaf of papers under her arm and wearing a look of great triumph. Hugo sat perched on her hat, looking pale but proud.

'Aaaah!' breathed the expectant company. 'Here they are.'

'Yep!' cried Pongwiffy, almost bursting with importance. 'Here we are – and the panto's finished, like I said it would be. And, what's more, it's all in poetry.'

'What's it called?' shouted Ratsnappy.

'It's called *Terror in the Wood*.'

Everybody tried it out. *Terror in the Wood*. It wasn't exactly traditionally pantomime-ish, but it had a certain something.

'I've got copies of everybody's part and I suggest that the first thing we do is have a read-through. I'll talk you through the story and when it comes to your bit, read it out. I shall be looking for volume, clarity and a deep sense of commitment.'

Pongwiffy bustled around the circle, handing out sheets of paper covered with spidery writing. Eager hands received them and heads bowed as everybody studied their part. She took her seat and

44

held up her hand dramatically.

'Right,' she said. 'Imagine it. The orchestra has played the overture. The stage is in darkness. The curtains part. Slowly, the lights come up on Sherlock Holmes's study. Enter Sherlock with his magnifying glass. Go on, Greymatter. That's you.'

'What about Speks?' said Greymatter. 'He wants to be in the panto too. Don't you, Speks?'

The small owl seated on the back of her chair agreed that yes, indeed, he would very much like to be in the panto.

'Not possible,' said Pongwiffy. 'There isn't a part for him.'

'He can play Watson,' insisted Greymatter. 'Watson, my faithful owl, who helps me with all my cases.'

'Watson wasn't an owl,' argued Pongwiffy.

'Sherlock Holmes wasn't an elderly Witch with a rather nasty perm, but that hasn't stopped Greymatter,' Sharkadder chipped in. 'Don't be mean, Pong. Let Speks be Watson.'

'Yes!' came several voices raised in agreement. 'Speks for Watson!'

Pongwiffy sighed. They hadn't even started and already people were arguing.

'All right,' she said. 'All *right*. Enter Sherlock Holmes with his magnifying glass and his ridiculous owl called Watson. Go on, Greymatter. Say your opening lines.'

'Ahem,' said Greymatter. 'Right. Er –

> *'And now at last our panto's done.*
> *We hope you had a lot of fun.'*

'I think you've got the pages mixed up,' said Pongwiffy stiffly. 'That's the end.'

'Oh – right. Sorry. Um –

> *'I'm Sherlock Holmes. How do you do?*
> *I'm searching for a vital clue.*
> *The Babes are missing in the wood –'*

She broke off as Agglebag and Bagaggle clutched at each other with excited little screams.

'That's us!' squeaked Agglebag. 'We're the Babes, Bag!'

'I know, Ag, I know! Oh my!'

'Shush!' Pongwiffy warned them sternly. 'No interruptions, if you please. Carry on, Greymatter. And try to sound less like a brick.'

Greymatter adjusted her glasses and carried on reading.

> *The Babes are missing in the wood.*
> *No news of them. This is not good.*
> *I have to solve this mystery*
> *Or those poor Babes is history . . .*

'Actually, Pongwiffy, that should read *are* history. Hope you don't mind my mentioning it.'

Pongwiffy gave a little frown.

'Well, all right, change it if you must. But I don't want you to think you can go round changing lines just because they don't suit you. We creative types can get very upset when people mess about with our work. It took me a long time to write this pantomime. Long, lonely hours, just me, my pen and my incredible imagination . . .'

'*Ahem!*' came a warning cough from her hat.

'Well, all right, Hugo helped a bit.'

'*AHEM!!*'

'A lot,' amended Pongwiffy hastily. 'Hugo helped a lot. Anyway, at this point you sing a jolly song, Greymatter, but we won't bother about that now. We'll move on to the next scene, which is set in a lovely woodland glade, with Snow White, Rapunzel and Sleeping Beauty dancing gracefully around a tree.'

'What?' chorused Sludgegooey, Scrofula and Bonidle, sounding startled.

'You heard. You've got to do a graceful dance.'

'What – now?' asked Sludgegooey. 'In front of everyone?'

'No, not now. We'll work on the dance another time. Just say your lines.'

Sludgegooey pulled her nose with filthy fingers and intoned:

> *'I am Snow White, as you can see,*
> *These are my good friends here with me,*
> *We laugh and play and have such fun*
> *And then we lie down in the splodge.'*

'What?' said Pongwiffy.

'There's an inkblot over the last word. I can't read it. What do we lie down in, Pongwiffy? After we've had all this fun?'

'Sun,' said Pongwiffy coldly. 'You lie down in the sun. It's obvious. It's got to rhyme with fun. Anyway, you'd hardly lie down in a cowpat, would you?'

'I might,' said Sludgegooey defensively.

'*You* might. But Snow White wouldn't, would she? You've got to stay in role. Right, your turn, Scrofula.'

Scrofula held up her sheet of paper and read:

> *'I am Rapunzel with long hair*
> *And Sleeping Beauty's over there.*

'How come my bit's shorter than Sludgegooey's?'

'And how come I don't get anything to say at all?' Bonidle wanted to know.

'Because you're asleep, of course,' snapped

Pongwiffy, beginning to sound exasperated. 'Anyway, you've got a line.'

'Have I? What is it?' asked Bonidle.

'"*ZZZZZZZZ*," ' said Pongwiffy. 'Now do it.'

Obediently, Bonidle did it. And that was the last they heard from her that evening.

'Right,' said Pongwiffy. 'On to the next bit. Sherlock Holmes questions the witnesses.'

'When does the fairy come in?' Sourmuddle wanted to know.

'Not yet,' said Pongwiffy through gritted teeth. 'Be patient, Sourmuddle, everyone can't enter at the same time.'

'I'm Grandwitch,' said Sourmuddle tartly. 'I can enter any time I like.'

'Not in a pantomime. You've got to wait your turn. Carry on, Greymatter.'

The great detective cleared her throat.

> *'Ah ha! Now, who is this I see?*
> *Three beauties dancing round a tree.*
> *Good morrow to Your Royal Highnesses.*
> *Excuse me while I –* clear my sinuses?'

Greymatter stopped, looking puzzled.

'Ah. That's where we have a bit of stage business,' explained Pongwiffy. 'You've got hay fever. You have to stop and blow your nose. It's the only word that rhymes with Highnesses, see. We were rather pleased with that bit, weren't we, Hugo? Carry on.'

> *'The Babes are gone! There is no trace!*
> *It is a most mysterious case.*
> *I wonder where those Babes can be.*
> *Oh, can you help, Princesses three?'*

There was a long pause. Macabre gave Sludgegooey an almighty nudge.

'Oh – is it me? Right. Um –

> *'We saw them pass a short while back.*
> *They went along that little track.*
> *They have been taken off by force*
> *By a Scottish woman on a horse.'*

'That's me,' Macabre informed everybody proudly. 'Hear that, everyone? Ma bit's comin' up soon.'

'What about the fairy?' demanded Sourmuddle again. 'I'm warning you, Pongwiffy, I'm not waiting much longer. It's the fairy that everyone's anxious to see, after all.'

'Dick Whittington is still conspicuous by his absence, I note,' remarked Sharkadder with more than a touch of pique.

'I think it's time the Pied Piper got a look-in, don't you, Vernon?' complained Ratsnappy.

'What about Cleopatra? clamoured Bendyshanks. 'Where's she, I'd like to know?'

'And another thing,' piped up Scrofula. 'What about Barry? If Sherlock Holmes can have a faithful owl, why can't Rapunzel have a faithful vulture?'

'It isn't possible,' explained Pongwiffy wearily. 'There just isn't room in this panto for all the Familiars. Those who haven't got a part get to do other things.'

'Like what?'

'Like scenery-shifting. And Noises Off.'

This statement was greeted by quite a lot of noises off, most of them raised in shrill complaint.

Pongwiffy and Hugo exchanged meaningful glances. It seemed that rehearsals were going to be a bit of a trial.

CHAPTER SEVEN

Preparations

Putting on a pantomime is not something that can be taken lightly – as Pongwiffy soon learnt.

To begin with, there was the question of music. The Witchway Rhythm Boys were the obvious choice, being local, so Pongwiffy went along to the specially soundproofed hut where they rehearsed.

'How much do we get paid?' enquired Arthur, the small Dragon who played the piano. (Dragons rarely become pianists, but Arthur was unusual. In fact, he was quite good, apart from an unfortunate tendency to set his instrument on fire during the faster passages.)

'What d'you mean, *paid*?' snapped Pongwiffy. 'This

 52

is a great honour, you know, being asked to perform in my panto.'

'We always get paid for gigs,' Arthur told her. 'Union rules.'

'Yeah, man,' agreed Filth the Fiend, Sludgegooey's Familiar, who played drums in his spare time. 'Gotta come up with the bread.'

'Toim's money,' nodded O'Brian, the Leprechaun, who played penny whistle.

'Well, I'm flabbergasted,' said Pongwiffy. 'Your self-ishness defies belief. After all the employment we Witches have given you in the past.'

'Yes, but we never got paid for it, did we?' Arthur reminded her. 'We're getting popular now. We can pick and choose. We've got the Skeleton disco next week and the Zombie barn dance and a Vampire ruby wedding Sunday fortnight. We're an up-and-coming band, we are. No pay, no play. That's the deal, right, boys?'

'To be sure,' said O'Brian firmly.

'You said it, man,' agreed Filth.

So Pongwiffy had to cough up.

Then there was the question of costumes. After a bit of thought, Pongwiffy decided to hire them. It virtually emptied the kitty, but costumes are one of the most important aspects of any production and Witches aren't known for their nifty work with a needle. She got Hugo to take everybody's measurements and sent off a list of requirements to Gentleman Joe's Theatrical Costume Hire Company, which advertised in *The Daily Miracle* and promised to deliver.

Then there was the scenery to consider. Pongwiffy engaged the services of a local artist, a Vampire by the name of Vincent Van Ghoul, who wore a red beret and matching smock and lived in paint-splattered squalor in the small shed he grandly called his studio. Vincent eked out a living as a portrait artist and welcomed the chance to do something a bit different.

'There are three scenes,' Pongwiffy told him. 'The first is Sherlock Holmes's study.'

'Great,' said Vincent eagerly. 'I'll paint it red. Nice vase of red poppies on the table. Bowl of tomatoes. That sort of thing.'

'The next is a woodland glade,' explained Pongwiffy.

'No problem,' said Vincent. 'I'll set it in autumn. At sunset. Nice red trees and a carpet of red leaves, I feel.'

'Hmm. And then there's the ballroom scene.'

'I see it all!' cried Vincent. 'Red velvet curtains with pots of red geraniums!'

That's the trouble with artistic Vampires, of course. They are red-fixated.

Then there was publicity to think about. There were posters to be designed. After a bit of thought, Pongwiffy came up with the following:

* * *

GRAND PANTOMIME
The Witchway Players
proudly present
TERROR IN THE WOOD
December 20 7.00 sharp
Witchway Hall –
Bring Your Fiends
(*STRICTLY NO GOBLINS!!*)

There were programmes to be printed and special invitations to be sent out to important people. Pongwiffy wrote a list of these, starting with royalty. The local Royal Family consisted of King Futtout, Queen Beryl and their daughter, Princess Honeydimple. They weren't particularly popular, but as their palace bordered Witchway Wood, it would have been unneighbourly not to send them an invitation.

Scott Sinister, the famous film star, was also down for an invite.

'I thought you'd gone off him,' Hugo reminded Pongwiffy, peering over her shoulder at the VIP list.

'So did I,' sighed Pongwiffy, 'but when it comes down to it, there is a corner of my heart that will be for ever Scott's. We've had our ups and downs, Scott and me, but that's what makes our relationship so excitingly special. I'm going to send him a handmade invite with "Don't Bring Lulu" at the bottom.'

(This will make sense to readers who have followed the previous exploits of Pongwiffy. If this doesn't include you – no matter. It is enough to know that Pongwiffy and Luscious Lulu Lamarre, the great actor's girlfriend, Do Not Get On.)

Other VIPs included Pierre de Gingerbeard (provided he was well enough) and the Yeti Brothers, Conf and Spag, who ran all the fast food establishments in the area. The only reason they appeared on the list was because Pongwiffy was rather hoping they might slip her a free pizza.

'Vot about ze Vizards?' Hugo reminded her.

'Oh, poo!' said Pongwiffy. 'What do we want silly old Wizards in the audience for?'

'Ronald vill be 'appy,' Hugo remarked. ''E don't vant it known zat 'e in Vitch panto. 'E don't vant to kiss Vitches. 'E sink all 'is friends vill laugh at 'im.'

'Good point,' said Pongwiffy, and promptly added the Wizards to the VIP list. 'They'll all have to pay though,' she added. 'The whole point is to raise money.'

Then, armed with a hammer and a mouthful of nails, she went scuttling off to pin posters to trees.

It wasn't really necessary. By now, word had got around. The Familiars had their hands full chasing away curious onlookers who crowded around Witchway Hall every evening, peering through the windows in the hope of getting a glimpse of rehearsals in progress.

And so the weeks went by in a dizzy whirl of activity – and almost before anyone realised it, autumn had given way to winter and the grand opening night was almost upon them.

CHAPTER EIGHT

Fancy Dress

Plugugly was skulking behind a bush down in Witchway Wood, straining to hear the conversation of two Skeletons who stood a short distance away, examining a poster displayed on a tree.

'Looks like the Witches are putting on some sort of show, darling,' remarked the first Skeleton. You could tell he was a male Skeleton, because he was wearing a bow tie.

'Hmm,' said his female companion, who was all decked out in a blonde wig. 'A pantomime, no less. Are we doing anything Saturday night, darling?'

'I doubt it,' said the other. 'Might as well go. Everyone else'll be there.'

'Except the Goblins, of course,' nodded the bewigged one. 'They're barred. The Witches won't let them attend anything these days. See?' She pointed a finger bone. '*Strictly No Goblins*. And quite right too.'

They laughed, linked arms and strolled on.

Ears burning, Plugugly hurried back to the cave to tell the others.

Eagerly, he burst in, blurting out, 'Guess wot? Dere's a pantymine, an' . . .'

'Ssssh!' said everyone.

All eyes were on Stinkwart, who was standing on a handy rock. He was wearing two large, branching twigs on his head and appeared to have reddened his nose with crushed holly berries.

'We're inspectin' each uvver's costumes fer the fancy dress ball,' explained Hog. 'We're tryin' ter guess 'oo we are.'

'Sorry,' whispered Plugugly and sat down. This was important. The bad news about the pantomime could wait.

'Right,' said Stinkwart. ''Oo am I?'

The Goblins stared with blank faces.

'Come on, come on,' urged Stinkwart. 'It's obvious, innit?'

Shrugs all round.

'Some kinda tree?' guessed Lardo.

'Nah, nah! Wassa matter wiv you? Look at the nose.

It's red, innit? So 'oo am I?'

'A red-nosed tree,' said Lardo. Once his mind was set on a certain course, it never deviated.

'Ah, to heck wiv it!' said Stinkwart, disgusted. 'I'm Rupert, ain't I? Rupert the red-nosed wassit.'

And he tore off his antlers, climbed off the rock and sat down in a sulk.

'I always thort it was Randolph,' said Hog to no one in particular.

It was Eyesore's turn next. He took his place on the rock, wearing what appeared to be an ancient bird's nest on his head. Bits of loose straw curled down to his shoulders. From his pocket, he took a tin bowl and a spoon. He batted his eyelashes, simpered and struck a pose.

'Right,' he said. 'Who am I?'

Another blank silence.

'I'll give you a clue,' said Eyesore helpfully. 'There's porridge in this bowl.'

Still no offers.

'I'm a little girlie,' prodded Eyesore. 'I'm a little girlie wiv long yellow hair an' I got a bowl of porridge. Oh, oh, I'm scared of the bears. Who does that remind you of?'

The Goblins were at a loss.

'Goldisocks!' exploded Eyesore at length. 'I'm Goldisocks, fer cryin' out loud. I got the wig an'

everythin'. Fancy not gettin' *that*.'

And he flounced off the rock in a huff, tossing his bird's-nest curls petulantly.

'Dis is no good,' burst out Plugugly. He simply couldn't help it. 'Dis is a waste o' time. Dere ain't no way we're gonna win de fancy dress prize unless we can come up wid somefin' better dan dis.'

'What about you, then?' demanded Eyesore, sullenly pulling his nest to pieces.

'Yeah, go on, Plug,' came the chorus. 'Wot's your costume, then?'

'I ain't got one,' confessed Plugugly lamely.

'Well, that's just great, that is,' said Sproggit spitefully. ''E picks 'oles in everyone else's costume, but 'e ain't even got one.'

Plugugly sighed heavily. In fact, he had thought a great deal about his costume. That's why he'd been loitering down in the Wood. He'd been trying to get some inspiration. He knew he wanted to be something spectacular, something that would cause jaws to gape and people to say things like, 'Good ol' Plugugly, trust him to come up with a Good Idea like that.' He could imagine himself receiving the prize from the Great Gobbo himself. He could visualise the thumps on the back, the cheers. He could see the scene. All he needed was the idea.

But he couldn't come up with one.

'Look,' he said. 'Look. I know you done yer best. I'm just sayin' we gotta do better dan dis if we're gonna win de prize. Dat's all I'm sayin'.'

'Know what'd be good?' said Slopbucket with a wistful air. 'Goin' an' buyin' ourselves proper costumes from a proper shop. That'd be good.'

'It would,' agreed Plugugly, ''cept dere ain't no proper costume shop round 'ere. An' even if dere was, we ain't got no money. An' even if we 'ad de money, dey wouldn't serve us, 'cos we's Goblins. An' dat reminds me. Dere's a Witch pantymine on Saturday night. Everyone's talkin' about it. Dere's posters all over de Wood. An' we's banned. I 'eard a coupla Skelingtons read it out. "No Goblins", dey said. Den dey larfed.'

'What's a pantymine?' Lardo wanted to know.

'I dunno,' confessed Plugugly. 'But I wouldn't mind de chance to find out.'

'It comes to somethin', don't it?' said Hog bitterly. 'No costumes, no money, no dinner an' banned from the pantymine. We must be the unluckiest Goblins in the world.'

They sat in a dejected circle.

'What we need is one o' them there things beginnin' with *co*,' said Stinkwart, very suddenly and very obscurely.

'What – you mean like a coconut?' said Lardo hesitantly.

'No, no. Longer. You know. When somethin' 'appens out o' the blue. One o' them flukes o' fate. You call it an amazin' *co* summink. It's on the tip of me teef. You know.'

'Well, person'ly, I ain't expectin' a coconut,' remarked Lardo, pleased with himself for having thought of one and not willing to let it go.

'Look, it's not a coconut, all right?' cried Stinkwart. 'It's – it's like when you got a fancy fer a big fruit cake, an' you ain't got one and then, just like that, there's a knock at the door an' there's yer granny! An' wot's she got in 'er 'and?'

'A coconut?'

'No, no,' began Stinkwart, beside himself with frustration. 'That's not wot I'm getting at –'

But he didn't get any further, because just at that moment there came a tentative knock at the front boulder. The Goblins jumped and looked at each other.

'Who's that, then?' hissed Eyesore.

'Probably Stinkwart's granny,' suggested Hog. 'And we were just talking about her too. What an amazin' coincidence.'

There was a loud clump as Stinkwart passed out on the floor.

'I hope she's brought the fruit cake,' crowed young Sproggit.

'And the coconut,' added Lardo happily.

Plugugly went to answer the boulder. Outside, it was sleeting. A small man with a whuffly moustache stood in a frozen puddle and touched his cap. A short way behind him was a large cart pulled by a bored-looking horse. Written across the side, in big, bold letters, were the words:

GENTLEMAN JOE'S THEATRICAL
COSTUME HIRE COMPANY

'Yeah?' said Plugugly. 'Whatcha want?'

'Sorry ter bovver yer, squire,' said the small man. 'Wonder if you can help me? I'm looking for Witchway Hall. I got an important delivery, see. Think I musta taken a wrong turn.'

'I think you must 'ave,' said Plugugly. 'You're right off track 'ere. Dis 'ere's Goblin Territory. You need a special secret password to go through 'ere.'

As he spoke, the rest of the Goblins came slinking up behind him.

'Wassee want, Plug?' asked Slopbucket.

''E's lost 'is way,' explained Plugugly. ''E's got a delivery ter make to Witchway Hall. I'm tellin' 'im 'e needs ter say de secret password.'

'Wot, you mean "Frogspawn"?' enquired Eyesore.

'Dat's de one,' agreed Plugugly. 'Right,' he added,

fixing the small man with a stern stare. 'Wot's de password?'

'Erm – frogspawn?'

'Correck. Right, you go down past de stingin' nettle clump, right, den you take a left, right, by de old cooker an' den a right, right? Or is it left?'

'Straight, innit?' interrupted Hog helpfully.

'Yeah, well, one o' dem. Den you follow de trail down an' around a bit an' den yer in de Wood. De Hall's in de middle somewhere. You can't miss it.'

'Thanks,' said the small man doubtfully. 'Very kind o' you, squire.'

'Dat's all right,' said Plugugly. 'Mind 'ow you go'. He watched him trudge away and climb into the driver's seat.

'By de way,' he called, 'by de way, wassit you're deliverin'?'

'Costumes,' replied the man, and clicked his teeth. The horse raised its eyes to heaven and lumbered off down the slope.

The Goblins looked at each other. They were too shocked to speak for quite some time. At last, Lardo spoke for all of them.

'Now *that*,' he said, 'is what I call an amazing coconut.'

CHAPTER NINE

Rehearsals

In Witchway Hall, a rehearsal was in progress. The current scene was a big, troublesome one, involving Lady Macbeth, half the Pantomime Horse, the lost Babes, Cleopatra, the Pied Piper, Dick Whittington and the fairy. As always, there was a lot of argument going on, mainly around the question of Lady Macbeth's transport. Macabre was flatly refusing to ride half a Pantomime Horse, claiming that she was a serious actress and it would make her look ridiculous. Gaga was prancing around in the wings, practising blowing through her nostrils.

'You've got to,' said Pongwiffy wearily. 'I've ordered the horse suit. I've written it in. Look, it's there in the script. "*Enter Lady Macbeth on half a Pantomime Horse.*" That's what Gaga wanted to be and I had to write her in somewhere. You don't want to do Gaga out of her part, do you? She's looking forward to it, aren't you, Gaga?'

Gaga snorted eagerly and pawed the ground.

'Lady Macbeth wouldnae ride half a horse,' objected Macabre. 'It's noo in her character. Anyway, it's noo possible tay ride half a horse. There has tay be a front end. For the reins.'

Pongwiffy sighed. The question of the horse's front end had been bothering her too. She kept pushing it away, hoping that a solution would present itself – but so far, none had. The trouble was, nobody wanted to be zipped into a dark, stuffy skin with an overexcited Gaga at their rear, doing goodness knows what. And who could blame them?

'Ah'm ridin' Rory,' announced Macabre. 'Ah always ride Rory. He's *ma* Haggis an' Ah'm ridin' him.'

Dead on cue, Rory trotted from the wings and stood shaking his orange fringe, doing his best fiery steed impersonation. Macabre climbed on his back and glared down stubbornly.

'All right!' snapped Pongwiffy, exasperated. 'All right, have it your own way. "*Enter Lady Macbeth riding a Haggis.*" Happy now? Don't worry, Gaga, I'll fit you in somehow. Tell you what, we'll give you a whole little scene of your own in front of the curtain. While the scenery's being changed. You can do a funny dance. All right?'

Gaga cantered in small, enthusiastic circles.

'Now, can we get on?' sighed Pongwiffy. 'Please? We've only got until Saturday, you know. Take your places on the stage, twins, and wait for your cue. Remember, you're tied together with rope. You've been kidnapped. You're frightened. Right, fire away, Macabre. Give it all you've got.'

Macabre fancied herself as an actress. She uttered a bloodcurdling cackle and shook her fist before launching into her big speech.

> *'The Babes are mine, there is no doubt.*
> *Ma wicked plan is working out.*
> *Ah'll tie them to this nearby tree*
> *So they cannae escape from me.*
> *Ah'm off tay write a ransom note*
> *And then Ah will come back to gloat.*
> *Ha, ha, ha!'*

'Very good, Macabre,' said Pongwiffy. 'Very sinister. Right, you tie the Babes to a tree, then go off to find a pencil. Go on, twins. It's your big moment.'

Agglebag and Bagaggle cleared their throats, clutched each other for mutual support, then spoke in chorus.

 69

> *'Alas! Alack! Oh, boo, hoo, hoo.*
> *Whatever can we poor Babes do?*
> *Oh, for a rescuer to come*
> *And reunite us with our mum.'*

And they looked at each other and giggled.

'Not bad, not bad,' said Pongwiffy. 'Try not to laugh, though. Right, now you lie down under some leaves and go to sleep and have a dream about Cleopatra. Where's Bendyshanks?'

'Here!' shouted the Queen of the Nile eagerly and bounded on. Slithering Steve was draped around her neck, doing his best to look like a poisonous asp.

'Say your bit, then,' ordered Pongwiffy.

> *'I'm Cleopatra from the Nile.*
> *I have a unique dancing style.*
> *So while the Babes enjoy their kip*
> *Sit back and watch me letting rip.'*

Bendyshanks then produced a tambourine and capered around the stage, doing a series of unusual leg-wavings. The twins forgot they were supposed to be dreaming and sat up to watch in fascination. Bendyshanks leapt about until she was purple in the face, then ended up doing the splits.

'So what d'you think?' she said.

 70

'You still need to work on it a bit,' advised Pongwiffy. 'Make it a bit more Egyptian. Try and be more exotic, Steve. Forget grass snake. Think python.'

'I was,' said Steve miserably.

'We'll try again, shall we?' asked Bendyshanks, eager as a puppy.

'No, no. Once is quite enough. We need to move on. Where are we in the script, Hugo?'

'"*Cleopatra exits to rapturous applause*,"' supplied Hugo doubtfully.

'Right. "*Enter the Pied Piper and Dick.*" '

'At last!' cried Ratsnappy and Sharkadder, hurrying on to the stage with Vernon and Dudley at their heels.

'What about the fairy?' piped up Sourmuddle testily. 'I've been waiting for ages. I am Grandwitch, you know.'

'Soon,' hissed Pongwiffy from between gritted teeth. 'She's coming on *soon*. Right, off you go, you two. Say your lines.'

Ratsnappy cleared her throat and stepped forward.

> '*You weren't expecting me, I'll bet.*
> *I'm the Pied Piper, with my pet.*
> *To comb this wood is our intent.*
> *We'll find those Babes, where'er they went.*'

She gave a deep bow and Vernon did likewise. Sharkadder elbowed them aside, swaggered forward with Dudley at her heels and slapped her thigh.

> *'And I am Dick, the hero bold.*
> *Full many a tale of me is told.*
> *I'm here to find those missing mites,*
> *With sword in hand and long green tights.'*

'Talking about tights, Pong, when are the costumes arriving? I can't quite get in role unless I look the part.'

'They're due to arrive this evening,' said Pongwiffy to cries of great excitement. 'But you're not allowed to wear them yet,' she added. 'Not until the dress rehearsal tomorrow. Right, let's get on, shall we? Start looking for the Babes. Off you go.'

Sharkadder and Ratsnappy began prowling about the stage, trying hard to avoid trampling over the twins' recumbent forms.

> *'No sign of them! Not one small clue!*
> *Oh, Dick, whatever shall we do?'*

declaimed Ratsnappy, treading heavily on Agglebag's finger. A most unBabe-like word came from beneath the pile of paper leaves.

72

> *'We must go on, that much is clear,*
> *Although I fear they are not here,'*

Sharkdadder informed her, stumbling over Bagaggle's foot.

Pongwiffy sighed. This was stretching the audience's credulity to the utmost limits.

'You're not supposed to discover them yet,' she explained. 'It's hardly very realistic if you keep tripping over them, is it? Right, Macabre, ready for your entrance?'

Macabre was. Mounted on Rory, she cantered on to the stage, brandishing a home-made cardboard sword.

> *'Aha! Ah know your cunning plan!*
> *You aim to foil me if you can!*
> *And then you'll make me take the blame.*
> *You hero types are all the same!'*

So saying, she dismounted and advanced upon the Pied Piper and Dick, whirling her sword around her head. The two bold heroes flinched and backed away uncertainly.

'Go on,' yelled Pongwiffy. 'Fight! This is a big action scene.'

'There's not enough room,' objected Ratsnappy. 'Not with Ag and Bag lying all over the place.'

 73

'Anyway, she's got a sword,' Sharkadder pointed out. 'We haven't got our swords yet. It's not fair.'

Macabre threw away her sword and adopted a boxing stance.

'Ah dinnae need a sword,' she informed them. 'Ah'll pulverise ye wi' me bare hands. Put yer fists up, ye pair o' softies.'

'That's not in the script, Macabre,' said Pongwiffy wearily. 'You're the baddy. You're supposed to lose, remember?'

But Macabre was enjoying herself. Her fighting spirit was up. She forgot she was supposed to be acting. Fantasy and reality became blurred and she advanced, fists flailing.

Ratsnappy hastily stepped back and tripped over Vernon, who collided with Dudley, who banged into Sharkadder, who fell heavily on to the missing Babes. Everyone went down in a heap and Macabre sat triumphantly on the top.

'There,' she said emphatically. 'That's got *that* sorted.'

'Does the fairy come on now?' enquired Sourmuddle plaintively.

Pongwiffy and Hugo looked at each other and raised their eyes to heaven.

'I think we've done this scene enough for today,' said Pongwiffy. 'Break, everybody. We'll all go home

for tea. But I shall expect you back here tonight at
seven o'clock sharp to rehearse the final scene. Yes,
Sourmuddle, that's you. We're going to do all the songs
and dances again as well. Make sure you're on time,
because I'm paying the Rhythm Boys overtime.'

There was a united sigh of relief and a surge
towards the door. Bendyshanks got there first.

'I say, everyone,' she said, peering out. 'Guess what?
It's snowing.'

And, sure enough, it was.

CHAPTER TEN

The Costumes Arrive

Now then. You may be wondering what has been happening to the small man all this time. The one who was bringing the hired costumes, remember?

Well, right now, sad to say, he is lost in the Wood. He was lost in the mountains earlier. And in the bog. He has spent hours and hours going around in circles being lost all over the place – and all because he'd followed Goblin directions.

On top of everything, it had begun to snow. Heavy white flakes whirled from the sky, obliterating the narrow path and dulling all sound. The dark trees were taking on a ghostly, skeletal look.

The small man's name was Ernest Dribble. He

 76

hunched miserably in the driver's seat, letting the horse pick its own way, while snow piled up on his hat and icicles formed on his moustache. Even worse – the last straw, this – he was getting the definite feeling that he was being followed. Whenever he slowed down, he heard cracklings and shufflings coming from behind him, and once there was the unmistakable sound of a nose being blown.

It was with a huge sense of relief that he suddenly rounded a corner and came upon a ramshackle building standing in the middle of a glade. Light streamed from the windows and from within came the sound of many voices raised in song, accompanied by a tinkling piano. At last! This must be Witchway Hall.

'Whoa, there, Romeo! Easy, boy!'

The horse ground to a sulky halt. Ernest Dribble climbed down, crunched across to the main doors, banged the snow from his hat and went in.

There was a short pause – then seven short, shadowy forms materialised out of the rapidly whitening bushes and swarmed gleefully over the cart like bees around a honeypot.

Meanwhile, inside the Hall, the final scene was in full swing. The Three Princesses had just finished another graceful dance, and Snoop was kneeling down with a hammer and a mouthful of nails, repairing the large hole

 77

in the stage. Everyone was gathered around the piano in the throes of the final song, except for Snow White, who was gloomily pulling splinters out of her foot.

'*If You're Happy and You Know It, Kiss a Priiinnnce,*' warbled the assembled cast enthusiastically. '*If You're Happy and You Know It, Kiss a –*'

'Hold it!' yelled Pongwiffy, raising her hand. 'Where *is* the flippin' Prince? He's supposed to be here.'

Everyone shrugged. Nobody had seen him.

'Perhaps he's snowbound,' suggested Sharkadder. 'It's getting very thick out there. You can hardly see a thing.'

'No excuse!' fumed Pongwiffy. 'No excuse at all. I *told* him. Seven o'clock sharp, I said, and ... yes, yes, what *is* it?'

She broke off to glare at a little man with a whuffly moustache who had suddenly appeared at her side and was trying to attract her attention.

'Are you Witch Pongwiffy?' enquired the little man, stamping his cold feet and shaking snow from his shoulders.

'I might be,' said Pongwiffy shiftily. She hadn't paid her gas bill for ages and was expecting a summons any day. 'Why?'

'Got somethin' for you,' said the little man, taking a piece of official-looking paper from his pocket. 'You gotta sign.'

'Well, it'll just have to wait,' said Pongwiffy. 'Right now I'm in the middle of a rehearsal. Sit down and don't interrupt. I'll deal with you when we get to the end of this very important scene. Oh, well, if nobody knows where Ronald is, we'll just have to carry on without him, I suppose. But I'm not happy. I'm not happy at all. Right, everybody. One, two, three!'

'*If You're Happy and You Know It, Kiss a Priiiince . . .*'

Outside Witchway Hall, the snow stopped falling as suddenly as it had begun. A pale moon swam into view, filling the glade with silvery light and making everything seem quite Christmassy. The only thing that ruined the effect was the sight of the Goblins ransacking the costume hampers.

'Cor!' hissed Eyesore, brushing off the snow and throwing back a lid. He reached in and yanked out a pair of silk pantaloons which were intended to grace the snake-like hips of the Queen of the Nile. 'Get a loada these drawers!'

'Look!' whooped Hog, snatching up Sherlock Holmes's deerstalker hat and ramming it on his head. 'Look at me, lads! I'm that there detectin' bloke! That there Shamrock Houses!'

'What about this, then?' gloated young Sproggit, throwing open another lid. 'Swords! Come on, boys, let's muck about!'

With cries of enthusiasm, everyone swooped on the cache of cardboard swords and began to muck about, as only Goblins can. All except Plugugly. He didn't move. He had found something wonderful in one of the hampers.

It was a horse suit.

It came in two halves which zipped together around the middle. It was white with huge red spots. The tail was made of raffia and the head came complete with large white cardboard teeth, pointy ears, a mane sporting a ribbon tied in a chocolate-box bow and a pair of huge, soulful eyes with the longest, curliest eyelashes you've ever seen.

'Whatcha got there, Plug?' asked Lardo.

'A horse suit,' whispered Plugugly.

Impressed by his awed tones, the Goblins dropped their swords and clustered round.

'Cor!' said Slopbucket. 'That's good, innit? Imagine if we went to the ball in that.'

'We can't all fit in,' said Plugugly. 'Dere's only room fer –' Carefully, he counted both bits. 'Two. Yes, two. One at de front and one at de back. An' I'm at de front,' he added firmly.

The two unoccupied front legs trailed limply on the ground as he cradled the head in his arms, stroking the mane and staring deep into the melting eyes.

'You're too fat,' announced Eyesore. 'You'll never fit in 'im.'

'Yes, I will,' said Plugugly. 'An' iss not a him. Issa her. She's got a bow, look.'

Carefully, he stepped into the dangling leg tubes and pulled them up, making sure he straightened all the creases. He then raised the head and lowered it over his own.

'How do I look?' came his muffled voice from inside.

'Good,' conceded Hog, with his head on one side. 'But there's somethin' missin', I dunno what . . .'

'The bum end!' shouted Sproggit, jumping up and down excitedly. 'You gotta have the bum attached, see, else it don't look right. Tell yer what, I'll be the bum. I'll put the back legs on, an' bend over an' grab Plug round 'is middle, then we can get the final effeck.'

And before anyone could say anything, he'd done it.

The Goblins had to admit that it looked good.

'Zip us up round the tummy, then,' came the muted instruction from the depths of the nether regions.

The Goblins hastened to oblige.

'Cor,' said Hog, standing back and admiring. 'That looks great, that does. Try movin' about a bit.'

The Pantomime Horse hesitated, then its front feet moved cautiously forward. There was a stretching effect in the middle of the body, followed by a sudden squeezed concertina effect as the two back legs careened forward in a shuffling little run.

'Oi!' protested Plugugly, as Sproggit's head cannoned into his substantial bottom.

'Don't go so fast, then,' protested Sproggit from the rear end. 'I can't see back 'ere. We gotta get a rhythm goin'. We gotta count. Er – wot comes after one again?'

'Two,' said Plugugly with the confidence of one who has worked that out earlier.

'Right. 'Ere we go, then. One, two, two, six, two . . .'

All this time, Romeo the carthorse had been standing stolidly between the traces, stamping the snow from his hooves and wishing he was back home in his warm stable, getting stuck into a nosebag. Now, however, he glanced over his shoulder – and did a double take. Hey! What was this? Another horse, no less! And, *phwoaaar!* What a babe! That exotic colouring – that cute bow – and, ooh, those eyes! Those melting, long-lashed eyes!

Eagerly, he shuffled round to get a better look.

Plugugly and Sproggit were beginning to get the hang of walking around in tandem now. It only took a bit of practice.

'Try trottin',' suggested Lardo.

Plugugly and Sproggit tried trotting. The front legs employed a sedate, high-stepping sort of gait, whilst the back legs kicked about in a skittish fashion. The watching Goblins clapped and guffawed. Say what you like, this was entertaining.

It was all too much for Romeo. This wasn't just a crush. This was Love. Yellow teeth bared in a soppy grin, he edged sideways up to his dream girl and playfully nibbled her ear.

'I say,' said Eyesore. 'I fink you got an admirer.'

'Eh?' said Plugugly from inside.

''E fancies you!' crowed Slopbucket, clutching his sides. 'You made a conquest there! Look, boys! The 'orse is in love!'

At this the Goblins laughed so much that they had to hold on to each other for support. Overcome with hilarity, they hooted and pointed and staggered around in the snow, tears streaming from their eyes.

But their glee was short-lived.

At that very moment, sudden light flooded the glade as the doors of Witchway Hall burst open – and out came Pongwiffy with Ernest Dribble scurrying in her wake!

'You should have told me you'd brought the cos- tumes,' Pongwiffy was saying. 'There was I, thinking you were from the Gas Board, and all the while –'

She broke off. She stared. She rubbed her eyes and stared again.

The Goblins, frozen in the light, stared back like rabbits who suddenly find themselves in the fast lane of the motorway.

It was Pongwiffy who broke the spell. Howling with outrage, she launched herself across the glade. With one accord, the Goblins dropped everything they were holding and took to their heels. The front end of the Pantomime Horse, having the advantage of limited vision, attempted to do the same. The back end, however, remained where it was. Sproggit hadn't a clue what was going on and nobody thought to tell him. The consequence was that the front legs did a lot of mad, panicky galloping on the spot, whereas the back legs had about as much forward momentum as a screwed-down table.

'Wot you doin?' squawked Sproggit's muffled voice.

'Wot's happenin'? Why you tuggin' me like that?'

'We bin rumbled!' wailed Plugugly. 'It's dat ol' Pongwiffy! She's seen us! Quick, Sproggit – run! One, two, six – keep in rhythm, for cryin' out loud – five, eight, nine . . .'

Crazily, they veered off into the trees. You might have thought things couldn't get any worse for them – but things did.

THUMP!

A crashing weight landed on top of them. They staggered and only just avoided falling to their knees in the snow.

'Hold it right there, gee-gee!' ground out Pongwiffy, wrapping her arms tightly around the Pantomime Horse's head. 'I said stop, d'you hear?'

'Don't stop!' gasped Plugugly. 'We can shake 'er off . . . keep goin' . . .'

And amazingly, despite the snow and the dark and the fact that they were bent double inside a horse suit with a very angry Witch on their back, they did keep going. And right behind them came Romeo, tugging the cart in his wake. His beloved had gone and he must follow! Hampers full of costumes came crashing down, spilling their contents into the snow as he galloped off in hot pursuit.

And that was the last anyone saw of any of them for quite a while.

CHAPTER ELEVEN

The Great Escape

Time now to move to another part of Witchway Wood, where another dramatic scene is taking place. This one is set in a mysterious cave – and it stars none other than Ronald!

He had come across the cave by chance some weeks earlier when he was plodding past on his way to yet another dreaded rehearsal, daydreaming about his Invisibility Serum and how it would change his life.

Poor Ronald. He hated rehearsals. Pongwiffy never got to his bit and he had spent every night for the past few weeks hanging around in the wings being ignored. It really is time he took a starring role.

The cave was set in a mossy bank and partially hidden

by the branches of a willow tree. He had noticed it out of the corner of his eye and gone to investigate. He was struck right away by its possibilities as a secret laboratory in which he could conduct his final experiment.

The cave had several advantages:

1. It would be more private. Things had been getting difficult back at the Clubhouse. The rumour had got round that he was doing secret research in his room and he was getting funny looks.
2. A cave was safer. You never could tell with Magic. Sometimes things could go a bit wrong. Noisy explosions might occur. There could be embarrassing side effects. Best to be on the safe side.
3. Magic worked better in caves. Things *looked* better. It was all to do with atmosphere – shadows, drips, echoes and stuff. Doing it in your bedroom with your teddy looking on just wasn't the same.

So, in the interests of privacy, safety and the look of the thing, Ronald had secretly moved all his paraphernalia to the cave in readiness for the first snowfall. Everything was there – the little jars and test tubes, the Bunsen burner and the crucible and so on, all set up ready and waiting, including a captive toad in a cardboard box with air-holes. Ronald was pretty sure that his serum would work – but he didn't fancy being the first to try it out.

 88

He had just started out for yet another rehearsal when the first flakes began to fall. Fresh Snow, at last! This was what he had been waiting for. Blow rehearsal. Blow princess-kissing. Blow everything. This was his Big Night – and nobody was going to take it away from him.

So, instead of making for Witchway Hall, he had made a beeline for his secret cave. Right now, he was on his knees, adjusting the Bunsen burner, waiting for his mixture to come to the boil. The flame was burning steadily and the serum was beginning to simmer. So far, so good.

The toad watched him unblinkingly from a nearby rock.

'Don't you move, mind,' Ronald warned it. 'Try and escape, and you'll be jolly sorry, I can tell you. I shall place a Spell of Binding on you that'll give you pins and needles for a fortnight. I don't really want to mix two spells up, because it might affect the results. But I will if I have to. What d'you say to that, eh?'

'Ribbit,' said the toad to that. Actually, it could speak excellent English but at this point it didn't want to commit itself.

'You're my guinea pig, you know,' Ronald told it.

The toad turned a pitying look on him. What was this idiot blithering on about? It was a toad. Anyone could see that.

Ronald turned back to the crucible and gave it a stir.

The mixture steamed. He sat back on his heels and watched it, cheeks red from heat and nervous anticipation.

'Know what this is?' Ronald asked the toad, who shrugged. 'It's my masterpiece. Extra Strong Invisibility Serum. And it's going to make me rich and famous.'

There was a pause.

'Ribbit?' said the toad, feeling that something was called for.

'Oh, yes. Really. One little sprinkle of this and *pff!* You're gone. Vamoosed. Disappeared. Vanished. Impressive, eh?'

The toad eyed the mouth of the cave and said nothing.

'Ha!' chuckled Ronald. 'I'll show those Witches they can't boss me around. I've got it all planned, you know. When they come looking for me, I'll just coolly sprinkle myself with the serum and vanish before their very eyes. Imagine their faces! And I won't show up again until after the pantomime's over. No more Prince Charming – and there'll be nothing they can do about it. Aha! We've reached boiling point. Get ready, toad. Snow Time!'

Eagerly, he rose to his feet, ran to the cave mouth and snatched up an old bucket which had been placed just outside to catch the falling snow. He hurried back, stepped up to the fire, adopted a suitably dramatic pose, lifted the bucket on high and solemnly intoned the

Magic words: 'Oggyoggyoggy! Oi, oi, oi! Come on, you serum!'

Then, with great ceremony, he upended the bucket and tipped the snow into the crucible. There was an almighty sizzling, a bang, a puff of purple smoke – and that was it. The crucible now contained a quantity of thin, colourless liquid with a slight oily sheen. Done. Finished. One Extra Strong Invisibility Serum. Now all he had to do was test it out.

Using an old tea towel, Ronald carefully removed the crucible from the heat, then turned to the toad with an unconvincing bedside-manner smile.

'Right,' he said. 'Sit still. This won't hurt a bit. I'm just going to sprinkle you.'

'Sprinkle yourself, pal, I'm gone,' said the toad. And with a huge leap, it shot over Ronald's head and out of the cave.

'Hey!' shouted Ronald, startled. 'You come right back here!'

Still holding the precious pot of serum, he raced from the cave and out into the snowy Wood.

And that was when things went horribly, horribly wrong. As he stood peering hesitantly around, there came the sound of howling. Crashing footsteps were heading his way. Startled, he looked up – and to his dismay, he saw five screaming Goblins bearing down on him on a collision course!

He gave a horrified gasp, took a step backwards in order to get out of their path – and his heel caught on a half-buried twig. Arms flailing, he tried to regain his balance as his feet slithered away from under him. The crucible flew from his hand. Up, up, it flew. Drops of precious liquid came raining down on the heads of the stampeding Goblin horde – and in a split second, before Ronald's very eyes . . . they disappeared! Simply twinkled out of existence. Just like that.

The only evidence of their passing was a line of jumbled footprints making off into the distance, accompanied by receding howls, like the wail of a runaway express train. Then even the howls dwindled away, and once again peace reigned.

Slowly – ever so slowly – Ronald sat up. He spat out a mouthful of snow and gingerly felt himself all over. His eyes flickered towards the crucible, which lay on its side in the snow. With a little moan, he flopped over on to his knees and crawled towards it. With a shaking hand, he picked it up and peered inside.

There was a spoonful left! Oh, thank you, thank you! All was not lost!

Sobbing with relief he staggered to his feet and turned back to the cave, clutching the crucible with its few remaining drops to his chest.

That was when he was hit in the back by a large, red-spotted Pantomime Horse.

CHAPTER TWELVE

The Show Must Go On

'I can't understand it,' said Sourmuddle, peering into her crystal ball. 'I should be able to locate them by Magic, but there's not a glimpse of them in my ball, and none of the Search and Find spells work. It's like the whole lot of them have vanished from the face of the earth. Highly mysterious.'

It was the following morning. The Coven, greatly excited by all the drama, had gathered at Witchway Hall for a hastily convened emergency meeting. Also present was Ernest Dribble, looking rather uncomfortable in his role of sole eyewitness to the dramatic events of the night before. There were rather too many pointy hats around for comfort.

 93

The only absentees were Hugo, Sharkadder and Dudley, who were presumably still out trawling the snowy Wood in a hunt for Pongwiffy. Either that or, as Sludgegooey unkindly remarked, home in their beds enjoying a few blissful hours without her.

'Tell us again what you saw, Mr Dribble,' ordered Sourmuddle.

'I told yer,' mumbled Ernest Dribble. 'It were Goblins. Them ones I seen earlier on. They musta followed me. They was over by the cart, muckin' about with the costumes, an' a couple of 'em 'ad the 'oss skin on, an' when they sees us they all makes a run fer it, an' then *she* goes an' takes a running jump an' lands on the 'oss an' they takes off into the Wood an' my Romeo, 'e takes off after 'em! 'E's a bit of a lad when it comes to the ladies,' he added, with a touch of mournful pride.

'Stupid, though,' remarked Sourmuddle. 'Seeing he can't even recognise his own species.'

'That don't stop me bein' fond of 'im,' snivelled Ernest Dribble. ''E's out somewhere in the cold, snowy wastes, eatin' 'is 'eart out, an' I miss 'im.'

He took out a grubby hanky and blew his nose.

'I don't know what you're moaning about,' remarked Ratsnappy. 'You've only lost a lovesick carthorse. We've lost a vital costume and our director, and it's opening night tomorrow.'

Everyone's stomachs flipped over at the thought.

'What are we going to do?' asked Bendyshanks worriedly. 'I mean, supposing Pongwiffy doesn't turn up? Who's going to organise tonight's dress rehearsal and tell us what to do and keep the Rhythm Boys in order and make all the decisions? Somebody's got to direct.'

There was an anxious silence. Even Sourmuddle looked uneasy. Grandwitch she might be, but when it came to the pantomime, Pongwiffy was the undisputed boss.

Bendyshanks asked the one question they were all privately thinking.

'Can we do it without Pongwiffy? Do you think we ought to cancel?'

'*Cancel?*' said a voice from the doorway, making everyone jump. '*Cancel?* Is you *crazy?*'

It was Hugo.

Eyes blazing, he scuttled down the aisle and up on to the stage. Everybody stared as he climbed on to Pongwiffy's empty chair and gazed sternly around at the assembled company.

'So!' he said scathingly. 'Is zis 'ow ve say sank you to Mistress for all 'er 'ard vork? Vun leetle problem and ve *cancel*? No, I tell you! No, no, no! She 'ave a dream, my mistress. She dream zat zis great show of ours vill pass into ze 'istory books! And now, just ven she need us most, you talk zis sissy cancel talk! Pah!'

There fell a guilty little silence. Everyone looked at each other.

Greymatter cleared her throat.

'Well, if you put it like *that* –'

''Course I put it like zat! So vot if Mistress gone missink? She turn up. Meanwhile, ze show must go on.'

'That's all very well,' said Sourmuddle. 'But who's going to direct?'

'Me,' said Hugo simply. 'Pongviffy, she say to me, "Ugo, if anythink 'appen to me, you must take over and be ze director." '

He crossed his paws behind his back. Actually, Pongwiffy had said nothing of the sort, but it was worth a try.

There was a bit of general muttering. His rousing speech had gone down pretty well on the whole, but the last bit was greeted with a mixed reception. There were some who weren't too happy at the thought of being directed by a Hamster.

'We'll take a vote on it,' decided Sourmuddle. 'Hands up who wants the show to go on?'

Everyone's hand shot up.

'And who thinks they can direct it better than Hugo?'

Hands dropped like leaves in autumn.

'That's it, then,' said Sourmuddle. 'Hugo's appointed

as the new director, and everyone has to do what he says except me, because I'm Grandwitch and I can do what I like.'

'But what about the costumes?' asked Sludgegooey. 'Some of them fell in the snow. They're all dirty. And a couple of the swords have gone soggy.'

'Ve vash ze costumes, ve fix ze swords,' said the new director briskly.

'But what about the Pantomime Horse?' piped up Bendyshanks.

'No problem. Ve cut it.'

'But what about Gaga? She doesn't have a part now.'

Everyone looked at Gaga, who had gone very small and sad, quite unlike herself.

'Ve find 'er sumsink else to do,' announced Hugo. 'She can be Usherette. Show people to zeir seats. Viz big, shiny torch. And sell ice cream at ze interval.'

It was an inspired suggestion. Instantly, a gigantic, sunny smile split Gaga's face. A big torch and ice cream! Hey! She could do a *lot* with those. She jumped up on her chair and performed a jolly little dance, then solemnly stood on her head.

'Nice to see her back to normal,' remarked Ratsnappy, and everyone agreed.

'So,' said Hugo. 'Is decided. Tonight, ve 'ave dress rehearsal as planned. And tomorrow night, ve open!'

Smiling and chattering, everybody pushed their

chairs back, ready to leave.

'Just a minute,' said Sourmuddle, holding up a hand. Everybody sighed and sat back down again. 'I'm as keen on the pantomime as the next person, but we can't just sit back and let those Goblins get away with it. I didn't get where I am today by letting Goblins get away with things. They have to be caught and punished in a proper manner.'

'She's right, you know,' muttered the Witches. 'They should be.'

'I'm not so bothered about Pongwiffy,' continued Sourmuddle, 'because I'm sure Hugo's right and she'll turn up sooner or later – but we have to get that horse suit back. It's a very expensive costume, and if it's lost or damaged, we have to pay for it.'

Just at that moment the door opened again. This time, it was Sharkadder. For some reason, she was looking terribly pleased with herself.

'Hello, everyone,' she trilled. 'Sorry I'm late. I've been on a very important mission. In fact, I've got the answer to all our problems. Meet Wildman Willy Racoon, famous tracker and bounty hunter and *my cousin*! Step in, Willy, and say hello.'

She stood aside. Behind her, arms folded and short, stocky legs akimbo, stood a Dwarf. He wore buckskin breeches, a fur-lined jacket and a pair of scuffed cowboy boots. On his head was a fur hat complete with dangling racoon tail. He wore a lasso looped over one shoulder and a musket over the other. His face sprouted the biggest, shaggiest mad tangle of a fearsome ginger beard that it is possible for a single face to support. It was the kind of beard things *live* in.

'Howdy,' said Wildman Willy Racoon.

Everyone goggled in surprise at the unexpected visitor.

'Willy's agreed to help us out,' explained Sharkadder airily. 'He's Cousin Pierre's twin brother. Haven't I ever mentioned him?'

'I don't think so,' said Sourmuddle doubtfully. 'I don't think we'll ever get to the bottom of your well of obscure relations, Sharkadder. Pierre's twin, did you say?'

'That's it. Pierre went into catering and Willy here went into – er – wild-manning. Didn't you, Willy?'

'Yup,' said Willy and spat on the floor.

'Yes,' continued Sharkadder. 'He lives up in the wilds of the Misty Mountains. Huntin', shootin' and fishin', isn't that right, Willy? Out in all weathers, sleeping under the stars, communing with nature, washing in icy mountain springs, eating beans and so forth. He came down to visit poor Cousin Pierre when he heard about the accident with the pancake mixer, didn't you, Willy?'

'Yup.'

'Doesn't say much, does he?' said Sourmuddle.

'Ah, well, he's not used to talking, you see,' explained Sharkadder. 'Up there in the mountains, all on his own with only the stars for company. Eating beans —'

'Yes, yes,' butted in Sourmuddle testily. 'I know about the beans. What I don't know is what he's doing here. We've got enough on our plate as it is without having to entertain your relations.'

'What's he doing here?' cried Sharkadder. 'Why, isn't it obvious? He's going to track down Pong and the Pantomime Horse, of course.'

'Zere you are, zen!' cried Hugo. 'Is all sorted.'

'And my Romeo?' chipped in Ernest Dribble eagerly. 'Can he find him too?'

'Certainly. He can find anything, can't you, Willy?'

'Yup,' growled Willy, adding, 'Ain't no critter can escape ma eagle eye.'

'It's true,' nodded Sharkadder proudly. 'He's quite a legend in the mountains. Show them your scars, Willy.'

The legend needed no encouragement. He rolled up his sleeve and pointed to his forearm.

'See this here? This here's where a mad ole grizzly took a chomp outa ma arm. An' this here's a gorilla's teeth marks. An' this here's where a fork-tongued poison-drippin' rattler sunked its fangs in ma wrist. Last bite that there varmint ever took. Ever eat rattlesnake? Tastes kinda scrumpchuss, all slaaaced up with a messa beans.'

At this, Slithering Steve gave a little shudder and quietly headed for the sanctuary of Bendyshanks's cardigan.

'Thank you, Mr Racoon,' said Sourmuddle briskly. 'I'm sure you're very experienced with wild animals. But this missing Pantomime Horse is quite another kettle of fish. I've tried all my strongest spells, but –'

'Magic! Ha!' Willy Racoon spat contemptuously on the floor again. 'Wildmen don't have no truck with that there sissy Magic. We got our own methods. I does it by sniffin' the wind with ma trusty conk an' inspectin' the ground with ma keen peepers. Ain't no critter can escape –'

'Your eagle eye, yes, you said. But there's another thing.' Sourmuddle peered sharply over her glasses. 'You call yourself a bounty hunter, so I take it you won't be offering your services for free. I'm afraid the funds won't run to –'

'Ah! That's the beauty of it!' cried Sharkadder. 'He's got no use for money, up there in the wilds, have you, Willy? He'll do it for beans! That's what you wildmen live on, isn't it, Willy?'

'Yup,' nodded Willy. 'An' snake. When we can git it.'

Bendyshanks's cardigan gave a convulsive little heave.

'You see?' crowed Sharkadder. 'Beans, that's what he likes. Normally, he charges two big sacks, but seeing as I'm family, we get a discount. One bag of beans and a free ticket to the pantomime. I've told him all about it and he's terribly excited. He's never been to a pantomime, have you, Willy?'

'Nope,' agreed Willy, adding hopefully, 'Will there be dancin' gals, did ya say?'

'Zere certainly vill!' burst in Hugo, thumping on the table in his excitement. 'Dancink girls and princesses and vicked Scotsvimmin and posh fairies, no less! Bring back my mistress and ze missing Pantomime 'Orse by tomorrow night, Villy, and ve vill give you a pantomime you vill never forget! Am I right?'

'Durn right!' came the excited chorus.

Wildman Willy's accent was catching.

CHAPTER THIRTEEN

The Powwow

'That,' said Slopbucket's disembodied voice, 'was the worst night of my life.'

From all around came grunts of heartfelt agreement.

There were five Goblins in the cave. You couldn't see them, of course. Only their voices gave a clue to their whereabouts.

'We'll be for it when them Witches catches up with us,' moaned Eyesore. 'They'll tan our hides for sure. If our hides ever come back again,' he added mournfully.

'It were scary, weren't it?' remarked Hog, with a shiver in his voice. 'Gettin' caught red-'anded like that.'

 103

'Not as scary as comin' over all invizdibibble,' whined Lardo. 'I don't like this 'ere invizdibibbility. Dunno what people see in it.'

There was a pause.

'They don't see nuffin' in it,' Eyesore's voice pointed out. 'That's the 'ole point.'

'All right, all right. I'm just sayin'. I miss meself. I wants me body back, even if it is a mass of bruises. You should see 'em.'

''Ow can we see 'em?' remarked Eyesore. 'They're invizdibibble.'

'That don't stop 'em 'urtin,' said Lardo.

It was true. In fact, all five of them were in a bad way. The long trek home on the previous night had been bad enough with the snow and the darkness to contend with, let alone the added handicap of invisibility. Not knowing where they began or ended meant that they continually misjudged distances and were forever bumping into trees, falling into snowdrifts and tripping over each other's invisible feet.

Goblins, however, have a built-in, primitive, pigeon-like homing instinct which comes to their aid at times of crisis. It works by overriding their brains. Just as well. They would never have got home if they'd relied on those. Even so, it had been well after midnight when they had finally made it back to their cave, where they had fallen in an invisible pile and instantly gone to sleep, hoping that everything would be better in the morning.

And now it was morning and everything wasn't.

'Wot I can't unnerstand is, 'ow did it 'appen?' said Hog for the hundredth time. 'One minute we wuz runnin' away an' the next, we wuz like this. 'Ow come?'

'Magic, innit?' said Slopbucket. 'Gotta be. Issa nasty ol' Witch spell.'

'Nah,' argued Eyesore. 'Wot'd be the point? The Witches wants to *catch* us, don't they? Now then. If you wants to *catch* sumfin', you don't make it vanish, do you? That makes it harder to *catch*, don't it?'

This was sound reasoning, for a Goblin.

'Who then?' pondered Hog.

There was a pause while the Goblins thought about this.

'P'raps it wuz that geezer in the pointy 'at,' said Stinkwart after a bit.

'Wot geezer in the pointy 'at?' enquired Eyesore.

'Remember when we was running across that glade? An' I wuz in front? There wuz a geezer in a pointy 'at come runnin' outa nowhere, straight into our path. I gotta kinda feelin' we mighta mowed 'im down. I didn't stop to check, mind, 'cos that's when I comed over all invizdibibble, an' everyfin' got confusin'.'

'Sounds like a Wizard,' observed Eyesore knowledgeably. 'Wizards wear pointy 'ats. 'E prob'ly done it outa spite, 'cos we mowed 'im down.'

There was a long pause, whilst the Goblins took this latest suggestion on board.

'P'raps we should find this 'ere Wizard an' throw ourselves on 'is mercy,' suggested Hog after a bit. ''E might take pity on us an' give us a wassit. You know. Wot yer mum gives you when you eats poison ivy.'

'A thump?' ventured Stinkwart, whose mum wasn't known for her bedside manner.

'Nah, nah. There's a word for it. Summin' what reverses the spell. You know. An anti – anti – 'ang on, it's comin' – anti –' You could almost hear his brain struggling – 'dot. Antidot!' he finished triumphantly.

'I got an Aunty Maureen,' remarked Stinkwart unhelpfully.

'Not the same,' explained Hog.

'I gotta niece,' chimed in Eyesore, not to be out-done. 'She's called Denise. I gotta nephew too.'

'What's 'e called?' asked Stinkwart.

'Denephew.'

'No good,' said Hog. 'It's gotta be an Aunty Dot.'

'Why?' argued Stinkwart. 'What can she do that my Aunty Maureen can't?'

''Ow should I know?' said Hog irritably. 'It's just somethin' I 'eard.'

'This isn't gettin' us anywhere,' said Slopbucket. 'All this talk of Wizards' aunties. When 'ave Wizards' aunties

ever 'elped out Goblins? Let's face it, lads. We're on our own. We'll just 'ave to sit tight till the spell wears off.'

'Well, let's 'ope it's soon,' put in Lardo. 'I'm 'ungry.'

'Tell yer sumfin' else wot's botherin' me,' said Hog suddenly. 'Where's Plug an' Sproggit? They ain't turned up, 'ave they? I thought they was followin' us.'

'They was!' cried Eyesore. 'I could 'ear 'em gallopin' along be'ind us, crashin' into bushes an' shoutin' at each uvver. I fink they was 'avin' trouble gettin' their legs sorted. An' that daft carthorse, 'e was comin' too, 'cos I 'eard 'im neighin'. An' then – an' then we was invizdibibble an' I dunno wot 'appened to 'em after that. I 'ad enuff problems of me own.'

'Fink we should get up a search party?' asked Slopbucket.

'Why?' said Lardo.

'Well – I dunno. Supposin' they're still stuck in the 'orse suit? They might be stufflecated by now. They might be in deadly peril, upside down in a snowdrift with their little legs wigglin'.'

The Goblins thought about this.

'Ah, they'll turn up,' said Eyesore after a bit.

'But wot if they don't?' persisted Slopbucket. 'Shouldn't we go lookin' for 'em?'

There was an even longer silence. Then: 'Nah,' said Stinkwart. 'Cold out there, innit?'

CHAPTER FOURTEEN

Up a Gum Tree

'Well!' said Pongwiffy disgustedly. She spoke with difficulty, on account of being suspended high in the air from a branch hooked into the back of her cardigan. 'This is a fine pickle you've got us into, I must say. Now we're *really* up a gum tree.'

They were too.

You may be surprised to hear that there are gum trees in Witchway Wood. But there are. There are oaks, ashes, elms, larches, sycamores, pines and gum trees. The gum trees are tall and thin and tend to be sticky.

The three of them had been up this particular gum tree for quite some time. The Goblins were still hopelessly trapped inside the horse suit. Plugugly was perched perilously astride a bendy branch which he gripped like a vice with his knees. Sproggit was lying stretched out behind him, belly down, hands hooked firmly on to Plugugly's belt, hanging on for dear life.

Above them dangled Pongwiffy, boots feebly paddling the air and hat over one eye.

Down below, Romeo circled the tree, swishing his tail and giving encouraging little whinnies. You could almost see the hearts coming out of his ears.

'Look at 'im!' groaned Plugugly. ''E don't give up, do 'e?'

''Ow can I look?' wailed the muffled voice of Sproggit. 'I ain't got no peep'ole. All I can see is your fat bum. Wot's 'e doin' now?'

'Grinnin',' said Plugugly, with a little shiver. 'Grinnin' up at us wid 'is spooky great teef. 'E loves us, Sproggit. 'E wants to go steady.'

'Shout at 'im,' suggested Sproggit. 'Tell 'im we ain't ready to commit ourselves to a serious relashunship.'

'Oi! Dobbin! Go 'ome! You ain't our type!' bellowed Plugugly, not very hopefully.

Romeo looked up and blew horsey kisses. Right now, his beloved was playing hard to get – but that was girls for you.

'It didn't work,' Plugugly informed his rear end.

'Well, I suggest you think of something that does,' ground out Pongwiffy from above. 'I've got to get down from here. It might have escaped your attention that I'm being strangled.'

'I ain't goin' down dere,' said Plugugly with a shudder. 'Not wid 'im down below, any rate. Catch me goin' down dere? Brrrr!'

'You got us up,' snapped Pongwiffy. 'You get us down. I really can't afford to hang around here any longer. I've got an important show to put on. I need that horse suit.'

'I's not gettin' down till '*e* goes,' repeated Plugugly firmly. 'An' if it comes to it, why don't *you* get us down? Cast a spell or summat.'

'That just goes to show how little you know about Magic,' sneered Pongwiffy. 'You can't just snap your fingers and hope it'll happen.'

(Actually, this is quite untrue. Any Witch worth her salt can snap her fingers and be sure it'll happen. All you need is a good memory and a headful of useful spells. The trouble is, Pongwiffy doesn't have either.)

'Call yerself a Witch?' jeered Plugugly.

'Certainly I call myself a Witch,' snapped Pongwiffy. 'It's just that I haven't got any of my stuff. At the very least I need my Wand. And how am I supposed to make a brew when . . . Oh. Oh dear.'

Suddenly, her voice changed. It now held an element of dread.

'Wot now?' said Plugugly.

111

'I think it's coming on again.'

Plugugly looked down and braced himself.

'She's right,' he said. ''Old tight, Sproggit. We're fadin'!' And he closed his eyes.

Things are getting complicated, aren't they? Pongwiffy, Plugugly and Sproggit are stuck up a gum tree and now they are becoming invisible. Perhaps we should take a step back to the night before and find out what led up to their current predicament.

There they were, racing through the Wood, with the Pantomime Horse running flat out and Pongwiffy bouncing about on top, grimly hanging on to the ears. When she had first taken that wild leap on to its back, it had been with the intention of stopping it. Now, with the besotted Romeo thundering along behind them, eyes rolling and steam issuing from his nostrils, she changed her mind.

'Faster!' she howled. 'Run, you idiots! Run!'

Luckily, the empty costume cart was proving to be a bit of a handicap to their pursuer. It kept getting stuck between trees, thus slowing him down a bit, otherwise they wouldn't have stood a chance.

Desperately, Plugugly and Sproggit pounded across the same glade that the advance guard of Goblins had raced through less than a minute previously. So great was their panic, and so limited was Plugugly's vision in the horse suit, that he didn't even notice Ronald, who

112

was just picking himself up from his first little encounter.

Pongwiffy didn't spot him either, because her hat was currently down over her eyes.

Yes, they mowed him down. And yes, as you might expect, they got sprinkled with the remaining drops of Invisibility Serum!

Good, you might think. What could be better, at times of crisis, than to become invisible?

Ah. If only it was as simple as that.

The trouble lay in the serum. There just wasn't enough of it. The first wave of fleeing Goblins had received a thorough drenching. Second time round, though, there was only a very little bit left – hardly a big enough dose to work effectively on one person, let alone three.

Pongwiffy, Plugugly and Sproggit didn't know this yet – but they soon would.

When invisibility first descended upon them, so blind was their panic that they hardly noticed. Plugugly and Sproggit had got so used to running that their legs just carried on pistoning up and down automatically for a bit. Then Pongwiffy became aware of a sudden, indefinable change. For a moment, she couldn't work out what it was. Then she looked down at herself – and saw fresh air!

'Hold it!' she screamed. 'Something's happened! We've vanished!'

At exactly that same moment, both halves of the Pantomime Horse became aware that something strange had occurred. They could see through the horse suit! They were still wearing it, they could feel it, but it had become transparent!

Even worse – so had they!

'Ahhhh!' shouted Plugugly, screeching to a stop. 'Where am I? I's gone! I can't see meself!'

Sproggit's invisible head once again thudded into the small of Plugugly's invisible back.

'Oooof!' remarked Plugugly conversationally as all the breath was knocked out of him. Down they both went into the snow, bringing Pongwiffy with them. All three flailed around, confused and completely unnerved.

'Where am I?' bawled Plugugly. 'Are you dere, Sproggit?'

''Course I'm 'ere. Where's Pongwiffy?'

'I'm here. Stop kicking me, will you?'

'Can you see me? I can't see me. I can't see you. Can you see you?' wailed Plugugly.

'Of course we can't see you!' snapped Pongwiffy. 'You've vanished. I've vanished. We've all vanished!'

'It's scary!' gibbered Sproggit. 'Wot's 'appenin'?'

As if things weren't bad enough, at that point Romeo came careering around the corner. He had finally shed his cart. One of the wheels had become wedged in a ditch and the traces had broken, leaving him free to pursue his darling to the ends of the universe. Further, if necessary.

He came to a halt, looking puzzled. Funny, there was no sign of her. Where had she gone?

'Ssssh,' hissed Pongwiffy warningly. 'It's him! Don't move!'

They sat in the snow, not daring to move a muscle, as Romeo stood hesitantly looking around. At one point, he stared directly at them – but after a heart-stopping moment or two, he gave a baffled little snort and began to move off into the trees.

'Phew!' said Pongwiffy, feeling invisible sweat break out on her invisible brow. 'That was close. Come on. Let's go while we get the chance.'

Shakily, they clambered to their feet – and at that point, without any warning, *they began to fade back in again*. First, there was fresh air. Then there was the ghostly image of a transparent Pantomime Horse and a see-through rider. Finally they were back, as solid as before.

'Hey!' shouted Plugugly. 'I'm back! Hello, me!'

'Quiet, stupid!' hissed Pongwiffy. 'D'you want him to hear?'

It was all too much for Sproggit, who finally lost his grip and began to scream.

Romeo stopped in his tracks. His ears pricked up

and he looked back over his shoulder.

There she was! His beloved! How come he'd missed her? With a wild neigh, he wheeled around – and once again the chase was on. The only difference was that the Pantomime Horse and rider faded in and out like a faulty television set. For a few minutes they would disappear completely, then they would materialise back again. And all the time, Romeo was gaining on them.

'Faster!' bellowed Pongwiffy. 'Go, go, go!'

'Plug!' screamed Sproggit. ''E's right be'ind me, Plug! I can feel 'is breath! I'm gettin' a stitch! I can't run no more!'

Desperate situations call for desperate measures. Plugugly saw the giant gum tree looming before him – and knew that this was their only chance.

'Quick, Sproggit!' he howled. 'Up de gum tree!'

And somehow – they never knew how – they made it.

So. Now we know where they are and how they got there. Many more long, argumentative hours stretch ahead of them. We could stay and keep them company – but we won't. Instead, we'll move forward a few hours and drop in on the proceedings in Witchway Hall, where the dress rehearsal is about to begin.

CHAPTER FIFTEEN

The Dress Rehearsal

In Witchway Hall chaos reigned. At the back of the stage, Vincent Van Ghoul was standing on a stepladder, hanging the first backcloth. This was of Sherlock Holmes's famous Baker Street study. It seemed that the great detective shared Vincent's fondness for the colour red. His study was painful to the eyes. Nobody liked to say so, though, with Vincent being an artist and all. The general consensus was, he'd been paid a lot so it must be good.

Elsewhere, nails were being hammered into cardboard trees. Chairs were being set in rows, with a great deal of scraping. In the orchestra pit, the Witchway Rhythm Boys were going through the overture. The din was unbelievable.

Hugo clapped his paws for silence.

'Right!' he squeaked. 'Leetle bit of 'ush now, if you pliz. All ze cast on stage and stand in line. Time for ze costume parade.'

With a bit of giggling and pushing, the cast filed in and lined up, looking rather self-conscious as Hugo moved slowly along the line.

The Babes were first. They were got up in frilly bonnets and large, matching sleepsuits. Agglebag's was blue and Bagaggle's was pink. Embroidered across the front on each, in large letters, was the word BABE. Each twin was sucking on a large dummy.

'Hmm,' said Hugo doubtfully. 'Perhaps ve should 'ave explained sings a bit more carefully ven ve ordered ze costumes. Oh vell. Too late now. Keep your tummies in and 'ope for ze best.'

Next came the Three Princesses – Snow White, Rapunzel and Sleeping Beauty – all got up in crowns and fancy frocks. In addition, Scrofula was wearing a straw-coloured wig which swept the floor and Bonidle was clutching a hot-water bottle.

'Vot zose stains on your dress, Sludgegooey?' asked Hugo sternly. 'Vot you been eatink in ze dressing room?'

'Beetroot doughnuts,' confessed the fairest one of all.

'Vell, don't. You s'posed to be Snow Vhite, not Slush Grey. 'Ang your 'air over your arm ven you is dancink, Scrofula, it could do somevun nasty injury. Vake up, Bonidle, you is droolink. OK, you vill 'ave to do.'

Bendyshanks was next.

'Hmm. I 'ope you is puttink cardigan over zat lot. Zat a lot of skin you is showink,' said Hugo.

'Ah,' beamed the great queen. 'Well, it's hot in Egypt, you see.'

'Not zat 'ot,' said Hugo firmly. 'Vear a voolly. Zat's an order. Zis is family show.'

Next was Sourmuddle – a vision of loveliness in spangly net. She did a couple of tottery fairy-like twirls, then sank into a creaky curtsy with one eyebrow enquiringly raised.

Everybody clapped politely.

'Ees good,' nodded Hugo. 'Ees very good, Grandvitch. But ze vings is upside down. And I should leave off ze boots.'

Sourmuddle looked shocked.

'Not wear my *boots*? But I always wear my boots. These are my great-granny's boots. They've been passed down from Grandwitch to Grandwitch, these boots.'

'It just zat zey don't quite go viz ze fairy image,' Hugo tried to explain. 'Fairies don't vear steel toecaps.'

119

'This one does,' Sourmuddle informed him crisply. So that was that.

With a little sigh, Hugo moved on to Sherlock Holmes.

Greymatter's checked cape and deerstalker hat were slightly the worse for wear, having been thrown into a snowdrift by Hog during his mad flight into the Wood.

'Excellent, Greymatter, excellent. You really do look ze part. I see your magnifyink glass is cracked. 'Ow you manage zat?'

'Accidentally, my dear Hugo,' explained Greymatter, who tended to talk in role ever since landing the part.

Hugo moved on down the line, where Sharkadder eagerly waited her turn for inspection. Her pipe-cleaner legs were encased in green tights and a feathered hat was placed at a jaunty angle on her head. She slapped her thigh, blew kisses and cried, 'My public, I love you, I love you all!'

'All right, zat'll do,' said Hugo. 'Your tights is all baggy vere your knees aren't. Pull zem up and stop hoggink ze limelight.'

'I don't see why I have to take orders from a Hamster,' muttered Sharkadder. But she said it quietly. Hugo was proving a very good director in Pongwiffy's absence. Everybody said so.

Next came Ratsnappy as the Pied Piper, clad in a headache-inducing cloak of many colours. She saluted with her recorder and stood to attention.

'Not bad, Ratsnappy. Just a *leetle* tip – try smilink. You ze friend of little children, ya? Zey love your merry music.'

Ratsnappy tried smiling. It didn't work. Her face just wasn't cut out for it.

Macabre was last. She bristled with cardboard weapons, looking quite terrifying in a floor-length tartan cloak. As Hugo approached, she threw back her head and cackled menacingly.

'Very nice, Macabre. Er – per'aps ve can do vizzout ze bagpipes. Zey might get in ze vay durink ze fight scene. Vere is Gaga?'

'She said she'd be a bit late,' said Snow White, absent-mindedly blowing her nose on the hem of her dress. 'She's practising with her torch.'

'Vot you mean, practisink viz 'er torch?'

'Well, she's borrowed all our kitchen chairs,' explained Rapunzel, 'and she's got them set up in rows. And she's making the Familiars be the audience and she's showing them to their seats. And if they don't do what they're told, she – er – practises with her torch. On their heads. It looks rather painful.'

'Fair enough. Right, 'ave I seen everybody? I got a feelink somevun missink.'

'There is,' said Cleopatra, bursting to tell. 'Ronald. He's still in his dressing room. We've told him to come out, but he won't. He says he's got a problem with his costume. He says he doesn't want to be Prince Charming and it's a silly old pantomime anyway.'

'Oh, he does, does he?' growled Sharkadder. 'Right, leave this to me. This is a job for Dick.'

She strode off in the direction of the dressing rooms. A moment later, everyone heard a thunderous banging.

'Ronald! Come out this minute, d'you hear? This is your aunty calling! Do you want a smack? You're not too big to be put over my knee, you know!'

There was a pause. Then there came the sharp sound of a foot connecting vigorously with wood, followed by splintering noises. Then came muffled voices, followed by the unmistakable sound of flesh connecting sharply with flesh. Seconds later, Sharkadder reappeared, looking pleased with herself.

'He's on his way,' she announced. 'It's amazing what a few kind words will do.'

Everybody looked expectantly towards the wings.

Poor Ronald. Things just weren't going well for him lately. As well as losing his Extra Strong Invisibility Serum, he was being made to dress up in a ridiculous Prince Charming outfit and make a fool of himself on stage. The only good thing that had happened to him recently was that he had been awarded his own dressing room. Hugo had explained that this was for two reasons:

1. He was the only male in the cast.
2. Nobody liked him.

Sulkily, he trailed on stage, clutching his reddened wrist. Everybody sniggered as he joined the end of the line.

'What's so funny?' he snarled.

'Your trousers, for a start,' said Snow White.

It was true. Not only were his breeches too big, the elastic had gone. He had had to tie them around his waist with string. Everything else was wrong too. The jacket was too small, the puffy-sleeved blouse was too long in the arms, his cardboard sword was floppy and his crown looked as though it had come out of a Christmas cracker and was perched on top of his sticky-out ears in a very silly way.

'Stand up straight, Ronald,' ordered Hugo. 'Prince Charmink not s'posed to 'ave caved-in chest. 'E supposed to look – 'ow you say? – dashink.'

'How can I?' cried Ronald, stamping his foot crossly. 'Nothing fits! I *gave* you my measurements. You must have written them down wrong. How am I supposed to look dashing in a dwarf's jacket and a giant's trousers?'

'It not my fault you got funny shape. And anuzzer sink. Vy vere you not at rehearsal last night?'

'I – um – got lost in the snow,' mumbled Ronald, going red.

'Vell, you should 'ave been 'ere,' Hugo told him sternly. 'Specially as ve 'ad crisis on our 'ands.'

'Dearie me. Did you?' asked Ronald innocently.

'We certainly did!' put in Cleopatra. 'The Goblins got away with our Pantomime Horse! Pongwiffy's out there somewhere, trying to get it back.'

'We've called in Professional Help,' added the fairy, sounding smug. Calling in Professional Help sounded rather businesslike. Sourmuddle liked to think of herself as the leader of the sort of Coven that, from time to time, might call in Professional Help.

'Oh, really? Who's that?' enquired Ronald.

'Cousin Willy,' burst in Dick. 'Remember Willy, Ronald? The wildman? Cousin Pierre's brother. He's your mother's sister's husband's uncle's grandma's nephew's third cousin twice removed by marriage. Lives up in the mountains. Eating beans.'

'Oh, yes,' said Ronald vaguely. 'Well, that's nice. Cousin Willy, eh? Well, well. How's he keeping these days?'

(Not that he cared. He didn't even remember Cousin Willy. He just wanted to draw the conversation away from the mysterious disappearance of Pongwiffy and the Pantomime Horse. He had a feeling that his role in the matter wouldn't be appreciated.)

'Look,' said Hugo. 'Look. Ve 'aven't got time for all zis. Ve got a dress re'earsal to get on ze road. Clear ze stage, everybody. Is ze orchestra ready?'

Various tootles, twiddles and smashings from the orchestra pit indicated that the orchestra was indeed ready.

'Right, boys!' squeaked the director. 'Off you go. Take it from ze top!'

CHAPTER SIXTEEN

Trackin'

Wildman Willy Racoon knelt in the cave, sniffing intently at the scattered ashes of a cold fire. All around lay a number of mysterious items. A box of matches. A Bunsen burner. The wrapper off a packet of Polos. A cardboard box with holes in. A host of little smashed pots, which rather looked as though somebody had hurled them at the cave wall in a fit of temper.

There was also a piece of many-times-folded paper, which had probably fallen from an inside pocket. It had been cut from a furnishing catalogue and contained a lot of information about chairs!

Willy Racoon prowled around some more. Behind a rock, he found another clue.

A pointy hat! It was rather battered and one of the stars was hanging on by a single thread. It looked as though someone had recently given it a good kicking.

Gingerly, he picked it up and peered inside.

'RONALD THE MAGNIFICENT,' read out Wildman Willy. 'WASH SEPARATELY. Hmm.'

He rolled up the hat and stuffed it into one of the pockets in his buckskins. Then, sucking noisily on a bad tooth, he walked to the cave entrance.

Just outside, the snow appeared to have been churned up by many feet. To add to the mystery, an abandoned copper pot lay to one side, half submerged in a snowdrift. You or I, not being skilled in the ways of the wild, wouldn't have known what to make of it, of course. Not so Willy. To his experienced tracker's eyes, the scene spoke volumes. It all pointed to a Magical experiment that had gone horribly wrong.

It was trusty-conk time again. Willy wiped his large, knowledgeable nose on his sleeve and snuffled at the air like a bloodhound.

'Durned if Ah don't smell Goblin!' he growled to himself.

Two rabbits watching from a nearby bush nudged each other.

'Who *is* that man?' breathed one.

'Don't you know?' whispered the other. 'That's Wildman Willy Racoon, the famous tracker! Ain't

127

nothin' can escape his eagle eye.'

The pair of them watched admiringly as Willy picked up the crucible, examined it, cautiously rubbed a filthy thumb around the rim and held it up.

'Wut in tarnation . . .' began Willy, starting back, his experienced wildman composure deserting him for a moment. He could see through his thumb! It didn't exactly vanish away completely – there wasn't enough serum left for that – but, for a brief moment, it became transparent!

The effect didn't last long. As he watched, the thumb faded back in and became solid again! Cautiously, he wiggled it, just to make sure. Yep. It was back all right, dirty as ever.

Then, suddenly, it all clicked. The clues added up to one thing.

'Ha!' he announced, slapping his thigh in triumph. 'Ah'll be jiggered! Durned if it ain't a case o' invisibility!'

'Amazing!' sighed the watching rabbits. 'How does he do it?'

Willy now turned his attention to the trampled snow.

There was a mass of footprints, some overlapping and some going off in confused little circles. It was clear that a major pile-up had taken place. As far as he could make out, there were seven – no, eight – sets of footprints leading off into the trees. Or, to be precise, six sets of footprints – and *two sets of hoofprints*!

The front set was big and rather silly-looking for hoofprints. The back set, which evidently belonged to a more conventional horse, was closely followed by two parallel lines which clearly had been made by a cart. Adopting a cautious, half-stooping gait, the legendary wildman followed the trail across the glade.

The two rabbits watched until he vanished into the trees. Then, in chorus, they both said, 'What a guy!' before skipping off back to their holes to tell their grandchildren.

Watching Willy work was indeed an education. Every broken branch, every overturned twig, every passing breeze told a story. Of course, it helped that there were footprints too.

At one point, the trail split. Without a moment's hesitation, Willy followed the tracks made by the hooves and the cart, which veered off to the right.

The trail went on, winding wildly between the trees. At times, Willy was up to his waist in snowdrifts – but this was routine stuff for someone who lives up in the Misty Mountains, eating beans.

Like a small, relentless snowplough, he plunged deeper and deeper into the Wood. At one point, he came across an overturned cart with one of its wheels firmly wedged in a ditch. From this point onwards, it became clear that the back set of hoofprints was gaining on the front set.

It was some time later, as he rested by a fallen log, eating a handful of beans to keep his strength up, that he heard plaintive cries in the distance.

'Heeeeelp!' came the cries. 'Heeeeelllllp!'

The scene at the gum tree was, in all essential details, exactly the same as when we left it – except that both Pongwiffy and the Pantomime Horse were now permanently visible. Much to their relief, the effects of Ronald's serum had finally worn off. It had taken a while, mind, and there had been some nasty moments. Fading in and out of sight has the same effect upon the system as riding up and down in a fast lift after a big dinner.

At the base of the tree, Romeo still waited patiently, kicking his heels and snorting sweet nothings. All right, so his new girlfriend had strange, foreign ways. Roosting up trees, for a start, not to mention her distressing tendency to fade in and out of sight. But in a way that made her more interesting. Anyway, she was back now, spotty and beautiful as ever.

'Heelllp!' Pongwiffy and Plugugly were bellowing in chorus. 'Heeeeeellllppp!'

There was a stubborn silence from Sproggit's end.

'What's he doing in there?' complained Pongwiffy. 'I don't see why we should be doing all the work. Oi! Sproggit! Help us shout, d'you hear?'

'Can't,' came the muffled squawk from the rear end. 'I've fainted. I can't 'old on no more. I'm finished, I tell yer.'

'No, yer not,' Plugugly told him. 'Yer gonna 'ang on tight. We's all in dis togedder, remember? We's all gonna –'

He broke off. Peering through the mouth hole, he had just spotted something. A small, determined figure in buckskins had suddenly stepped out from behind a bush and was striding towards them, deftly twirling a lasso.

Romeo looked around, startled.

'Whoa, boy,' the stranger was saying soothingly. 'Now then, now then, eeezy does it, eeeeezy does it . . .'

There was a whistling sound, the spinning rope snaked through the air – and plopped neatly over Romeo's head.

Romeo let out an outraged whinny and reared up on his hind legs. What was this? Captured, just as he was about to become engaged? Never!

'What was you sayin', Plug?' came Sproggit's anxious voice.

'Eh?'

'You said we wuz gonna do somethin'.'

'Fall,' said Plugugly tiredly. 'I was sayin', we's all gonna fall.'

With that, Romeo's flailing front hooves lashed out,

catching the trunk of the gum tree, which shuddered under the impact.

'EEEEEEEEE . . . .' went Pongwiffy.

'NOOOOOOOO . . . .' went Plugugly.

'AAAAAAAH . . . .' went Sproggit.

And the Pantomime Horse toppled from its branch and came plummeting down on to Romeo's broad back like a sack of potatoes.

And, seconds later, on top of *it* – *plumph*! Down came Pongwiffy.

The effect on Romeo was electrifying. He looked around and his ears pricked up. He could hardly believe his good fortune. At last, his darling had relented! Oh joy! Now he could carry her off to his stable and show her his horse brasses. All he had to do was get rid of the pesky Witch and the even peskier Dwarf on the end of the rope.

Nostrils flaring and mane tossing, off set Romeo at a mad gallop, Pongwiffy and the Pantomime Horse help-lessly flopping and bouncing about on his back as they were borne off on yet another ghastly stage of their adventure.

And behind, flat on his bottom, clinging grimly to the length of rope, came the legendary wildman, the heels of his boots ploughing up great sprays of snow as he was tugged relentlessly ever onward.

CHAPTER SEVENTEEN

Overture and Beginners

The inhabitants of Witchway Wood tend to be somewhat tribal in their habits. Skeletons stick with Skeletons. Trolls tramp round with Trolls. Ghouls go round in gangs. Tree Demons hang out with other Tree Demons and so on. The only thing that prompts the various factions to bury their differences and mingle is the prospect of live entertainment. Stick up a poster advertising any sort of show and you can guarantee that they'll all come crawling out of the woodwork.

The prospect of a pantomime proved irresistible, particularly on a wintry Saturday night with a huge moon shining on the snow and the smell of Christmas in the air. The Wood rang with the chattering voices of excited theatregoers, all wrapped up warm and making for Witchway Hall, which Vincent Van Ghoul had decked out in red fairy lights for the occasion.

On the edge of the glade, five invisible pairs of Goblin eyes watched from behind a handy clump of snow-covered bushes.

'Come on, then,' hissed Hog's voice. 'Are we goin' in or what?'

'Not yet,' said Slopbucket. 'We don't wanna draw attenshun. We gotta wait till everyone's gone in. Then we'll sneak in at the back.'

'You sure this is a good idea?' piped up Stinkwart, sounding doubtful.

'Wassamatter? You don't wanna see the pantymine?'

'Yeah, yeah, 'course I do. But s'posin' we gets caught?'

''Ow can we get caught? We're invizdibibble.'

There was a pause. Then: ''Ow come we're sneakin' about be'ind bushes, then?' asked Stinkwart, He had a point.

'Traditional, innit?' said Slopbucket. 'We're Goblins. Goblins always sneak about be'ind bushes. Anyway, stop bein' a wet blanket, Stinkwart. At least we're 'avin an outin'.'

'Oh, yeah,' said Stinkwart glumly. 'I fergot I was 'avin fun. Sorry.'

'There's only one fing I'm sorry about,' chipped in Hog, sounding pious. 'I'm sorry that our good ol' mates

Plug an' Sproggit ain't wiv us. Don't seem right, us out enjoyin' ourselves when they're stuck in a snowdrift with their legs wigglin'.'

There was a long, rather guilty silence.

'Ah, they'll turn up,' said Eyesore.

'You keep sayin' that,' Hog reminded him. 'But they 'aven't, 'ave they?'

'Anyway,' said Slopbucket uncomfortably. 'Anyway, we 'ad to get out, didn't we? All that lyin' low wuz doin' my head in.'

Lying low had indeed proved to be more than the Goblins had bargained for. Hour after hour after hour of sitting in a gloomy cave staring at the space where your body should be can get to you.

It had been Lardo who cracked first. He had suddenly shot to his invisible feet, announced that he was feeling claustrophobic and that if he didn't get out of there immediately he wouldn't be responsible for the consequences. Well, he didn't actually use those words. They were much too long for a Goblin. What he actually said was, 'Ahhhhhh! Lemmeoutlemmeoutlemmeout!'

At any rate, he put into words what everyone else had been thinking for some time, and it was the signal for a mass exodus.

If you had been an innocent bystander, you would have seen the boulder door roll to one side, a slight rippling effect in the cold air and five pairs of footprints suddenly appear in the snow. But that's all. As yet, Ronald's serum was showing no signs of wearing off. The Goblins were still well and truly invisible.

Outside, as the long shadows of evening crept across the snow, they stood and debated what to do next.

'Now what?' asked Hog. 'Can't stay 'ere all night.'

'I knows wot we can do,' said Slopbucket suddenly.

'Wot?'

'We can cheer ourselves up an' go on a little outin'.'

'You mean, like, the seaside or summink?' enquired Eyesore doubtfully. Even if he had any swimming trunks (which he didn't), he wasn't sure he could find them at such short notice. Besides, it was hardly seaside weather.

'Nah, nah. Look down there, lads. Whadya see?'

The Goblins looked. Far below, in the darkening Wood, there was a red glow. It lit up the snowy tops of the surrounding trees in a rather festive way. It appeared to come from the general area of Witchway Hall.

'Know what's 'appenin' tonight?' said Slopbucket, his voice all wobbly with excitement. 'The pantymine! What do ya say, lads? Fancy a spot of entertainment?'

'We mustn't!' gasped the others. 'We're not allowed in.'

'Ah,' said Slopbucket gleefully. 'Ah. But they can't stop us, can they? 'Cos we's invizdibibble. Come on, lads. Foller me!'

His footprints set off at a run down the slope – and

after a moment, four more sets took off after him.

And that is how the Goblins came to be skulking around in the bushes, waiting for the right moment to slip in and enjoy a night of *Terror in the Wood*.

Backstage, in the dressing room, hysteria reigned as first-night nerves set in. The Babes had lost their dummies. Dick Whittington, having just redone her make-up for the seventeenth time, had suddenly discovered a ladder in her tights and was having a temper tantrum in a corner. Snow White had spilled an entire tin of rouge down herself and was trying to get it off using a cup of cold bogwater and Cleopatra's wig. Rapunzel's lethal hair was tripping everyone up, its owner included. Sourmuddle's wings were giving trouble.

'My wings won't stay on! Who's got the safety pins?'

'There's a ladder in my tights! A ladder, I tell you!'

'I've lost my recorder! How can I play merry music without my *recorder*, for mercy's sake!'

'Has anyone seen my wig?'

'Ouch! Mind where you're putting that sword, Macabre . . .'

Sherlock Holmes hadn't a clue where she'd left her magnifying glass. Sleeping Beauty's hot-water bottle was leaking. Barry was in the toilet, being sick again – and he was only Noises Off!

Suddenly, without any warning, the call came. There

was a knock at the door and the announcement came that set hearts pit-pattering and stomachs churning.

'Overture and beginners, please!'

There was an appalled silence.

'Oo-er,' said Bendyshanks. 'That's torn it. Too late to back out now.'

Next door, all alone in his dressing room, Prince Charming stood before his mirror, eyes starting out of his white face and all ten fingers stuffed in his mouth in an attempt to still his chattering teeth. He was currently suffering from a shocking attack of stage fright. Despite all his efforts at keeping his theatrical activities under wraps, somehow his fellow Wizards had got to hear about them and the entire Clubhouse had promised to come along to cheer him on. He had thought the previous night had been the most embarrassing of his whole life. Now he wasn't so sure.

On the stage, peering through a crack in the curtains, Hugo stood alone, watching the seats fill up. It looked like it was going to be a packed house. Mistress would be pleased – if only she was here to see it. Anxiously, he took out a tiny pocket watch and examined it.

Three minutes past seven. Time for curtain-up.

With a little sigh, he put the watch away. It looked horribly like she wasn't going to make it.

CHAPTER EIGHTEEN

Terror in the Wood

Imagine it. The packed hall. The audience rustling and whispering in delighted anticipation. A single spotlight trained on the closed curtains.

Snug in the warm darkness, a row of Wizards are noisily tucking into huge bags of popcorn. A small Thing in a Moonmad T-shirt is absent-mindedly eating his programme. A Skeleton hiccups, and everyone sniggers, apart from those who have had the misfortune to have fallen foul of the overenthusiastic Usherette. They are nursing their sore heads and moaning quietly.

Everybody is present and correct. Pierre de Gingerbeard, the famous chef (twin brother, of course, to our old friend Wildman Willy Racoon), has managed to struggle along, despite his injuries. The Yeti Brothers have taken a rare night off and are sitting munching pizza next to a row of Banshees.

Also present is a Gnome called GNorman; a couple of Mummies, with freshly laundered bandages put on specially for the occasion; a small, portly Genie by the name of Ali Pali, who is trying to sell a carpet to the large Troll sitting next to him; somebody called Mrs Molotoff, who is wearing a lot of fruit on her head and is apparently a seaside landlady; Mr Molotoff, who is called Cyril and is carrying a vacuum cleaner; Ernest Dribble, still grieving for the absent Romeo but not enough to go out there looking for him; one Dunfer Malpractiss (shifty-looking owner of the local Magic shop); and a rather bad-tempered Tree Demon who is refusing to share his fruit drops with *anybody*.

The Royals are there too. Worried little King Futtout sits sandwiched between his vinegar-faced wife and his pouting daughter, who has a face like thunder. Honeydimple hates Hamsters, Witches and Pantomimes, in that order.

One of the Mummies leans over, taps King Futtout on the shoulder and demands that he remove his crown. King Futtout hurriedly does so.

Just along from the royal party sits Scott Sinister, star of stage and screen. He is yawning hugely and ostentatiously looking at his watch, even though it's dark. He wishes to make it very clear that he does not want to be here. He has not brought Lulu.

Suddenly, at the back, in a blast of cold air, the doors creak open, then shut themselves again.

And now, at the very back, where there is standing room only, *there are five invisible Goblins*! But nobody knows that yet.

Down in the orchestra pit, Filth picks up his sticks and plays a drum roll. Arthur plays a series of menacing chords, which are meant to conjure up visions of dark doings and wicked deeds. O'Brian puts his penny whistle to his lips and plays something altogether different, because he's got his music in the wrong order.

Time to begin. The curtains wobbled back, giving everyone a wonderful view of Vincent Van Ghoul's paint-splattered rear end as he bent over making some last-minute adjustments to the vase of plastic poppies on Sherlock Holmes's desk.

The audience gave a united gasp at the redness of it all. Those who had brought them hastily put on their sunglasses.

'Van Ghoul!' hissed Hugo's voice urgently. 'Get off!'

Vincent turned around, gave a startled little squeak and scuttled out of sight. The audience sniggered and delightedly nudged each other. It was a good start.

On came Sherlock Holmes, Watson perched on his shoulder. Both looked horribly nervous, as anyone would be who had to start the whole thing off. Greymatter raised her trembling magnifying glass, inspected the audience and muttered something.

'Mumble mumble mumble do?
Mumble mumble mumble clue.'

'What's the funny man say, Mummy? shrieked a small Banshee very clearly from the back row.

Greymatter cleared her throat and tried again.

'Mumble mumble mumble do . . .'

'Speak up!' yelled a Mummy impatiently. 'We can't hear you.'

Greymatter glared. 'I *said*, cloth-ears, that I'm Sherlock Holmes, how do you do, I'm searching for a vital clue. And I'll thank you to keep your mouth shut, sonny. Some of us are trying to act up here.'

The audience clapped. This was more like it. There was nothing like a bit of heckling to get everyone into the spirit of the thing.

In command now, the great detective went on to explain the business of the missing Babes and his own personal role in the matter. He did it so movingly that several members of the audience wept into their hankies.

'Is ze rhyming couplets,' muttered Hugo to the Three Princesses who were waiting nervously in the wings. 'Gets 'em every time.'

Throughout Greymatter's speech, Watson nodded encouragingly and made admiring noises, which is, of course, what the Watsons of this world are born to do.

At the very back, the five invisible Goblins were struggling to get to grips with it all.

'Wassappenin'?' hissed Lardo, nudging Hog in his invisible ribs. 'Wot's 'e sayin'?'

'I dunno. Summink about some missin' kiddies.'

'Wot kiddies? Why they missin'?'

''Ow should I know?'

'Sssssh!'

A Zombie sitting in the back row turned around crossly, intent on telling off whoever was making all the noise. Seeing nothing but fresh air and shadows, he looked puzzled, then turned back to face the stage.

Greymatter finished her speech and stepped to the front of the stage. Hugo pulled on the rope and the curtains closed behind her. The Witchway Rhythm Boys struck up an introductory bar or two, and a large piece of cardboard descended from the wings with words on it. It narrowly avoided decapitating the great detective, who leapt out of the way just in time. To her credit, Greymatter recovered quickly and launched into her song.

We have not heard this before, so we should give it a listen, as Hugo is particularly pleased with this song. It is set to the tune of 'Oh, I Do Like to be Beside the Seaside', and right now Greymatter is giving it her all.

'*Oh, I do like to be a great detective,*' she trilled, enthusiastically conducting the audience with her magnifying glass, while Watson pointed to the words.

> '*Detecting's the thing I like to do,*
> *There is nothing I like more*
> *Than hunting on the floor*
> *Where I might just find*
> *A puzzling clue, clue, clue . . .*'

'Listen to zem!' crowed Hugo. 'It goink vell, ya?' But the Three Princesses were too nervous to talk.

> '*Oh, I do like to be a great detective,*
> *Detecting's my specialiteeee,*
> *I can solve the hardest crime*
> *In a record-breaking time,*
> *Need a detective? Then call for me!*'

The song ended, to rousing cheers. Glowing with triumph, Greymatter and Speks made their exit.

The Woodland Glade scene came next. The curtains parted and the onlookers were treated to yet another faceful of Vincent Van Ghoul's visionary scenery. More gasps of astonishment at the beauty of it all.

The Three Princesses stood in a circle, holding hands. The band struck up something vaguely skippy, and Sludgegooey, Scrofula and Bonidle rolled their eyes and proceeded to thump around a cardboard tree while the audience watched in fascinated disbelief.

At the end of the dance, there was a storm of delighted applause. Dripping with sweat, the Princesses grinned sheepishly and stared uncertainly into the wings, unsure what to do.

'Do it again!' mouthed Hugo. 'Go on!'

So they did it again. And got another round of applause.

They would have done it a third time, but the stage was beginning to splinter and Hugo signalled that enough was enough. With a sigh of relief, Bonidle slumped in a pile of paper leaves and promptly went to sleep, as the part demanded.

As soon as Snow White and Rapunzel had rather breathlessly introduced themselves, on marched Sherlock Holmes and Watson. Their earlier triumph had given them real confidence. Greymatter's business with the hanky was particularly compelling viewing and got a cheer.

146

'Acting at its finest,' whispered one Ghoul to another.

When the great detective had unblocked his nostrils to his satisfaction, he enquired about the Babes and received the information that they had been taken off by force by a Scottish woman on a Haggis.

'I knew ve should have vorked on zat line,' sighed Hugo to Vincent Van Ghoul, who was watching from the wings. 'It just not ze same, some'ow.'

It didn't matter. Out front, the audience were lapping it up. All except the Goblins. They were in a state of bewildered outrage.

''Ear that?' spluttered Eyesore. 'Some Scottish woman's got them kiddies! Poor little nippers.'

'Ssssh!' said Lardo. 'Snow White's talkin'. I don't wanna lose the thread.'

'But some Scottish woman's taken a coupla babies from their mammy . . .'

'I know, I know.'

'Sssshhh!'

Up on stage, Snow White was suggesting to Sherlock Holmes that he call in a couple of professional heroes to help on the case.

> *'Dick Whittington will help you out,*
> *Of that I'm sure there is no doubt.*
> *I also might suggest to you*

You call in the Pied Piper too.
Why don't you give them both a ring?
But now, I think it's time to sing.'

The Witchway Rhythm Boys hastily put down their cups of tea, snatched up their instruments and played the opening bars of the next song. Snow White, Rapunzel and Sherlock Holmes linked arms and sang from the footlights. Bonidle stayed where she was, sleep-singing.

'Rock-a-bye, babies, gone in the night
Maybe to Scotland, hope they're all right . . .'

Everyone joined in, even the Wizards, who weren't known for their community singing. When the song reached its conclusion, there was hardly a dry eye in the house. The curtains closed, the house lights went up and it was time for the interval. Gaga, clad in her Usherette's uniform (consisting of a natty little hat teamed with a swirly skirt and, rather oddly, yellow wellington boots), hurtled down the aisle bearing a tray.

With one accord, the audience leapt to their feet and swooped on the ice cream.

CHAPTER NINETEEN

More Terror

As intervals go, it was a great success. There had been several interesting scuffles in the ice-cream queue and at one point the Usherette had been required to perform yet more vigorous work with her torch. As the lights went down for the second act, everyone hurried back to their seats, eager to find out what would happen next.

The Goblins, of course, hadn't dared go for ice cream. Not only would they have been trampled in the rush, but there was the distinct possibility that food eaten by an invisible body might well remain on view. Five splodges of chewed-up goo floating in the air didn't bear thinking about. Instead, they had whiled away the interval mulling over the events of the first act. Indignation kept their minds off their empty tummies.

'Wicked, I calls it,' Hog was saying in a hoarse whisper. 'Stealin' 'elpless liddle kiddies away from their mammy . . .'

'What's the world comin' to, I wanna know?' agreed Eyesore. 'We should do somethin'. We should form a search party.'

'Wot, like the one we didn't form when Plug and Sproggit went missin'?'

'Yeah, but this is different. This is liddle *kiddies* we're talkin' about 'ere . . .'

'Sssh. It's startin'.'

There was an ominous roll of thunder, the curtains jerked apart and Lady Macbeth rode on stage, bristling with cardboard weapons and hauling the Babes behind her on the end of a long rope. She reined in centre stage, glared at the audience and uttered a wild laugh, just in case anyone was in any doubt about whether or not she was a baddy.

> '*Ha, ha, ha, ha, ha, ha, ha, HA!*'

The entire audience erupted in a cacophony of boos and hisses.

'It's her!' squawked Lardo, quite beside himself. 'It's

that Scottish woman! The cheek of it! She's got the Babes! There they are, look!'

'Get her! The Scottish one! She did it!' howled Hog.

'You leave them Babes alone!' bellowed Stinkwart.

'Yeah!' screeched Slopbucket. 'Stop bullyin' them Babes, you wicked ol' woman, you!'

Luckily, everyone else was making such a noise that nobody noticed the racket from the back.

Enjoying herself, Macabre delivered her big speech with lip-smacking relish, tied the twins to a cardboard tree and strode offstage on a quest for a pencil.

'I don't believe it,' moaned Eyesore. 'They've let her go!'

It was Agglebag and Bagaggle's big moment. They removed their dummies, rolled their eyes at each other and lisped their lines.

'Alas! Alack! Oh, boo, hoo, hoo.
Whatever can we poor Babes do?
Oh, for a rescuer to come
And reunite us with our mum.'

'Aaaaah,' snivelled the mothers in the audience. 'Poor little dears. Shame.'

Looking rather pleased with themselves, the twins lay down at the foot of the tree and buried themselves under a pile of red-paper leaves.

This was the cue for Cleopatra's dream sequence. The lights dimmed, the Witchway Rhythm Boys struck up with something snake-charmerish, and Bendyshanks hurtled on stage with Steve coiled dramatically around her neck. The exotic effect was slightly spoilt by the addition of a woolly cardigan, but even so she made the audience sit up.

In ringing tones, she informed everybody that she was Cleopatra from the Nile and that she had a unique dancing style, which she was about to demonstrate.

'Who's this?' whispered Hog, struggling to get a grip. 'What's she doin' 'ere?'

He wasn't the only one. The confused audience rustled their programmes and whispered amongst themselves, not quite keeping up with the subtleties of the plot. Nobody could work out what an Egyptian queen in a woolly cardigan was doing in the Wood at this particular stage in the story.

It didn't really matter, of course. All that mattered was that the dance was entertaining. Bendyshanks gambolled energetically around the stage, pointing her toes and rattling her tambourine, with Steve clinging on for dear life. It was a thoroughly abandoned performance. At one point, she got so hot, she removed her cardigan, hurling it wildly into the audience, where it was caught by Mrs Molotoff's Cyril, who took it home for a souvenir. The audience cheered like billy-o,

153

and it all went straight to Bendyshanks's head. Next to come off was her wig, which was batted around a bit before being neatly fielded by the Thing in the Moonmad T-shirt, who ate it. She would have gone further, but caught sight of Hugo sternly shaking his head. So she contented herself with a final leap or two before sinking into the splits with a tearing sound. She got a nice round of applause, more for enthusiasm than anything else.

With a little yodel, the Pied Piper came bounding on, Rat at heel.

> *'You weren't expecting me, I'll bet.*
> *I'm the Pied Piper, with my pet.*
> *To comb this wood is my intent*
> *We'll find those Babes, where'er they went.'*

'I should jolly well fink so too!' said Slopbucket disgustedly. 'Time someone did summink. Who's this skinny geezer comin' now?'

On strode Sharkadder with Dudley in tow, waving her sword and slapping her thigh and declaring that she was Dick, the hero bold. The four of them then commenced prowling about the stage, pointedly avoiding the pile of leaves hiding the missing Babes.

This was all too much for the Goblins. Why, it was patently obvious where the Babes were hiding. How could anyone not see it? They simply couldn't contain themselves any longer.

'They're behind you!' screamed Lardo, jumping up and down in an agony of frustration. 'You stupid or what?'

'Yeah!' chimed in Hog. 'I can see their liddle tummies, look, pokin' out from them leaves!'

'Behind you!' shrieked Stinkwart. 'Behind you! Behind you! Behind you!'

With one accord, both cast and the entire audience turned around to see where the heckling was coming from.

It should have been all right, of course. After all, the Goblins are protected by their invisibility, right?

Wrong. Whatever the reason – whether it was overexcitement, the heat of the theatre, the fact that all spells wear off in time or simply plain old bad luck – at this extremely critical moment, just when the Goblins had rashly drawn maximum attention to themselves, *the serum began to wear off*!

'Behind you!' they were screaming. 'Behind you! Behind you! Behi—'

Suddenly, they became aware of all eyes on them. Their voices tailed off. They looked down at themselves, then at each other. They were back again. Hopelessly solid as ever. As visible as visible can be.

'Oooops a dandelion!' said Slopbucket.

On stage, all action had stopped. Dick Whittington and the Pied Piper stood rooted to the spot, their mouths forming identical Os. Aware of the sudden silence, the missing Babes emerged from their pile of leaves and sat up.

You've probably heard the expression 'It Never Rains But It Pours'. Consider what happened next.

The floor began to shake and from outside there came the unmistakable sound of approaching hooves. The door burst open with a crash – and there, framed in the doorway, was Romeo, looking overtired and sulky. Mounted on his back was the small, triumphant figure of Wildman Willy Racoon. In his hand he held a rope. Tied to the end, looking very much the worse for wear and drooping with exhaustion, was the missing Pantomime Horse. And sitting on *its* back was . . .

'Mistress!' whooped Hugo ecstatically, throwing his script in the air. 'You back! Hooray!'

And he ran from the wings, down the stage steps, scuttled up a red-spotted leg, up Pongwiffy's arm and on to her shoulder, where he proceeded to throw his paws around her neck.

'You take over,' he begged in her ear. 'It all too much for me.'

'Cousin Willy!' squealed Sharkadder. 'You see? I told you he'd find them!'

'Well, I never!' gasped the Goblins. 'It's Plug an' Sproggit!'

'Romeo!' cried Ernest Dribble, leaping from his seat. 'Romeo, Romeo! Where's your cart now, Romeo?'

'I dun it!' shouted Willy. 'I got both yer hosses back. Have Ah missed the dancin' gals?'

By now, the word had spread backstage and the entire cast came pouring from the wings.

'What's happening?'

'Pongwiffy's back! With the Pantomime Horse!'

'That's not all! There's Goblins in the theatre!'

'Where?'

'There, look! Up at the back!'

'They've gatecrashed our pantomime!'

'*Let's get 'em!*'

The pantomime was forgotten as the entire cast poured from the wings and down the stage steps into the auditorium. The Goblins clutched at each other and rolled their eyes in panic in the face of the advancing tide. Then:

'HOLD IT RIGHT THERE!'

The voice had authority. It rang out, clear and strong. Everybody hesitated and looked at the stage. There stood Pongwiffy, face grim and arms akimbo. At her side was the Pantomime Horse, looking rather sheepish (if it's possible for a horse to be sheepish) and swaying slightly in the spotlight.

157

'Zat's right, you tell 'em, Mistress!' urged Hugo from her shoulder. 'Break a leg!'

'This will not do,' announced Pongwiffy. 'It's always the same, isn't it? Everything always ends in chaos. I come up with these exciting ideas, just to brighten up our humdrum lives a bit, you know, and there's always some disaster. Well, this time, it's not going to happen, see? I'm back now and I'm taking over. Me and Hugo here have written a lovely pantomime and you're jolly well going to enjoy it. Dribble, remove that wretched horse. Everybody else, simmer down. If you're not in the pantomime, get back to your seats. Actors, get backstage and wait for your cue. Wildman Willy, keep an eye on those Goblins and make sure they don't escape. They're under house arrest. I'll deal with them later. But right now, there's a show going on. Do it. NOW!'

Everyone was so surprised, they did it. The audience obediently took their seats and the cast meekly began to shuffle back towards the stage.

'And while everyone's getting themselves settled,' continued Pongwiffy, 'the Pantomime Horse will entertain you. With a dance.'

'Eh?' came two startled voices from inside the horse suit.

'You heard,' muttered Pongwiffy out of the corner of her mouth. 'This is show business. Dance. Or else.'

Raising her voice, she shouted, 'We all want to see the horsey dance, don't we, boys and girls?'

'Yes!' came the thunderous response.

'Then, music, maestro, please!'

The Witchway Rhythm Boys looked at each other, shrugged and struck up with a jolly version of 'Yankee Doodle'.

There was nothing else for it. Plugugly and Sproggit took deep breaths, picked up their leaden feet and began to dance. And, what's more, they did it *well*.

As the tune picked up speed, their tiredness fell away and suddenly each found he had a spring in his step and a song in his heart. Legs coordinating beautifully, the Pantomime Horse kicked up its heels and skipped about the stage with its tail swishing and its head held high.

At the end of the routine, its front legs crossed and it gave a deep bow.

The audience went wild.

'More!' they shouted. 'More!'

It would be nice to say that the Pantomime Horse's dance was the highlight of the show. But it wasn't. Not quite.

The fight between Lady Macbeth, Dick Whittington and the Pied Piper proved very exciting, and the goodies triumphed, of course, although the general feeling was that Lady Macbeth won on points. Then, a mysterious fairy turned up and gave everyone three wishes, which was very nice. It was a pity her wings fell off, but most people were polite and pretended not to notice. She was the Grandwitch, after all.

When Sherlock Holmes finally found the missing Babes and everything was sorted out to everyone's satisfaction, the entire cast took to the stage for the final rousing song. The whole thing reached its grand climax when Prince Charming, brick red with embarrassment, trailed on stage and, to the great delight of the watching Wizards and his own everlasting shame, awarded each of the smirking Three Princesses a grudging peck on the cheek.

Yes, of course his trousers fell down. They'd have to, wouldn't they?

When the howls of glee finally began to die down, Greymatter stepped forward and delivered the closing lines.

> *'And now at last our panto's done.*
> *We hope you had a lot of fun.'*

'Hooray!' roared the crowd. 'We did! What a show!'

'Author!' yelled the Thing in the Moonmad T-shirt. And everybody else took up the cry.

'Author! Author!'

It was music to Pongwiffy's ears. She walked on

stage, Hugo sitting proudly on her hat.

'Thank you!' she cried. 'Thank you, one and all. As some of you may know, this pantomime has had its fair share of problems. But I think for once I can safely say that everything ended happily ever after.'

The cheers rose to fever pitch.

'Hugo,' said Pongwiffy, 'I think this is my finest hour.'

And, so saying, she stepped over the edge of the stage and fell like a stone into the orchestra pit.

CHAPTER TWENTY

Christmas Eve

'Snowing again, I see,' said Pongwiffy. 'You'll have to shovel the path, Hugo. After you've cooked my supper.'

'Ya, OK,' said Hugo. He was standing on a step-ladder, putting the finishing touches to the Christmas tree. The Broom stood below, handing up the tinsel.

'I want a proper invalid supper, mind. Maybe a little soup, or a lightly poached egg.'

'Ya, ya, OK.'

'Shouldn't those mince pies come out of the oven now? Actually, skip the invalid stuff. I'll just make do with those.'

'You 'ave to vait. Zey not ready yet.'

'But I'm hungry!' wailed the invalid. 'I haven't eaten a thing since teatime. I've got to keep my strength up.'

''Ave some leftover skunk stew. Zere's a big pot of it under ze sink.'

'I don't fancy it,' grumbled Pongwiffy. 'It's months old. There's green speckly bits in it. I want mince pies and I want them *now*.'

'Ya, ya, OK, *OK*! Vait a minute, vill you? 'Ugo, do zis, 'Ugo, do zat. 'Ugo, don't forget to 'ang up my stockink, 'Ugo, put anuzzer log on ze fire, 'Ugo, pop out and buy some more Christmas cards. You not sink I got enough to do?'

'Ah, but I've got a broken leg.'

'Zat not my fault.'

'Yes, it is. You said, break a leg. And I did.'

'I keep tellink you! Break a leg is old theatrical sayink. It not mean you got to go and do it!'

Pongwiffy had, indeed, broken a leg. It was the left one. Right now, she was sitting in her favourite rocking chair with her leg heavily encased in plaster and a crutch lying across her lap. On Christmas Eve too.

A knock came at the door and the Broom swept over to open it. A flurry of snowflakes blew into the hovel along with Sharkadder, who was carrying a large sack over her shoulders.

'Surprise! Hello, Pong. I've brought you your Christmas present.'

163

'Really?' Pongwiffy looked more cheerful. 'What's that, then, Sharky?'

'Well, you're not supposed to open it until tomorrow, but as you're poorly, I'll let you. Here.'

She dug into the sack and withdrew a parcel wrapped in old newspaper.

'Oh,' said Pongwiffy. 'Gift-wrapped, I see.'

She unwrapped it and held up a large, shapeless, sludge-coloured cardigan.

'It's hand-knitted,' explained Sharkadder. 'I hope you like the colour.'

'Oh, I do, I do. Sludge. Lovely. Just like the other hand-knitted sludge-coloured cardigans you've given me for the last fourteen Christmases.'

'I thought you could wear it to the big Christmas lunch at Sourmuddle's tomorrow,' explained Sharkadder. 'Twelve o'clock prompt, mind. Don't forget. Everyone's invited. We're all bringing something. Cousin Willy's bringing beans and Cousin Pierre's made us a lovely Christmas pudding.'

'I've got some nice leftover skunk stew,' began Pongwiffy, but Sharkadder shook her head.

'Oh, no, Pong. You're the guest of honour, on account of the wonderful job you did with the pantomime. We've raised loads of money, you know. Anyway, you've got a poorly leg. How *is* it feeling?'

'It hurts,' said Pongwiffy with a sniff. 'It hurts a *lot*.

There's only one thing that's cheering me up.'

'And what's that?'

'I don't hurt as badly as the Goblins,' said Pongwiffy with a little chuckle.

'I was going to ask you about that. I know Sourmuddle said you could decide on their punishment, to make up for all the suffering they caused you. So what did you do with them?'

'I turned them over to Gaga,' said Pongwiffy with malicious pleasure. 'She practised on them with her torch.'

Over in the Wizards' Clubhouse, the Wizards sat in overstuffed armchairs before a roaring fire. A row of stockings was pinned hopefully to the mantelpiece. There was a general air of seasonal festivity. Boxes of chocolates, heaped bowls of candied fruit and little glasses of smoking green stuff were very much in evidence.

The door opened quietly and Ronald slipped in, trying to make himself as inconspicuous as possible. He had kept himself to himself since the night of the pantomime. He couldn't face all the teasing and jokes at his expense. He had made the excuse of a bad cold and had stayed in his chilly attic room, eating his meals off a tray.

However, it was Christmas Eve and the sound of

165

clinking glasses and rumbling laughter had finally drawn him down to the lounge. He rather hoped that his acting debut would have been forgotten by now. He would just slip quietly in and warm his hands before the fire for five minutes . . .

'Hey!' shouted Frank the Foreteller. 'If it isn't Prince Charming! Where've you been keeping yourself, Your Royal Highness?'

'I've had a cold, actually,' muttered Ronald.

'Oooh dear, sorry to hear that. Probably caught something from all that princess-kissing, eh?'

He gave a wink and everybody but Ronald fell about in paroxysms of wheezy laughter.

'Look,' said Ronald bitterly. 'Look, I don't want to talk about it, all right? I'm not going to spend my whole Christmas being the butt of your jokes. Now, if you'll excuse me, I shall retire to my room . . .'

'Hang about, hang about, keep your hair on. What d'you think, gentlemen? Shall we give it to him now?'

'Yes, go on,' urged Dave the Druid. 'Let him have it. He needs cheering up.'

For the first time, Ronald became aware of a large, gaily wrapped parcel sitting in the middle of the lounge.

'For me?' he said.

'For you,' chorused the Wizards.

 166

'We had a whip-round,' explained Fred the Flameraiser.

'Go on,' urged Gerald the Just. 'Open it.'

So Ronald opened it. He ripped off the fancy paper, removed the top of the box and peered inside. What he saw caused a lump to form in his throat and tears of gratitude to well up in his eyes.

'Oh,' he said. 'Oh. Thank you so very, very much. It's just what I always wanted.'

It was a chair. A chair of his very own. It had a carved back. It had a cushion with tassels on. It had a plaque with his name on. Ronald the Magnificent, it said.

It rather seemed that Christmas wasn't going to be so bad after all.

Far away, somewhere in the Lower Misty Mountains, lies Gobbo Towers, home of the Great Gobbo. Tonight, there is something special going on. A fancy dress ball, no less.

The Great Gobbo sits on a raised dais at one end of the great hall. You can tell this is the Great Gobbo, because his braces are made of gold thread and he wears a crown over his bobble hat. He is also being fed grapes by a bevy of Goblin handmaidens in pink bikinis, just like Lardo described.

The floor is packed with Goblins of all shapes and

sizes. They have been dancing the night away to hideous sounds provided by the Goblinaires – an enthusiastic trio whose instruments consist of a burglar alarm, a dustbin lid and a blackboard (for scraping the fingernails down).

The time has now come to judge the fancy dress competition. The Great Gobbo claps his hands for silence and runs his eyes over the massed ranks before him. It is not a promising sight. There is only so much you can do with twigs and birds' nests. The place is packed with Randolph the red-nosed wassits and Goldisockses.

Only one Gaggle of Goblins stands out from the rest. At least their costumes are original.

They are covered in bruises. At least three have black eyes and two have cauliflower ears. Bandaged limbs and sticking plaster are much in evidence. It all looks terribly realistic.

The Great Gobbo crooks his finger. The bandaged ones start and, uttering things like, 'Who, us? Does he mean *us*?', hobble painfully to the dais, where they stand awestruck before their great leader.

The Great Gobbo picks a grape pip out of his teeth and surveys them in silence for a moment. Then he speaks.

''Oo you s'posed ter be, then, lads?'

The one with the badly dented saucepan on his

head clears his throat nervously.

'As you can see, Great Gobbo, we has made a group effort. We has come as a Gaggle o' poor, innocent Goblins who, through no fault o' deir own, has got tangled up with a loada spiteful ol' Witches. We has come as a dreadful warnin' to you all. We calls ourselves the Dreadful Warnin' Boys. Sir.'

'I like it,' said the Great Gobbo. 'It's different. It's new. It don't involve twigs. I award you first prize.'

He waved his hand and a huge hamper was ceremoniously brought on and dumped at the feet of the incredulous winners. When the lid was raised, it was found to contain a year's supply of tinned nettle soup!

'Oh, wow!' gasped Plugugly, quite overcome. 'Dis is too much! Some Christmas dinner iss gonna be dis year, lads.'

It was only when they got home that they realised they didn't have a tin opener. But that's another story.

Time now for the happy ending. What could be nicer than Witchway Wood on this Christmas Eve, with the snow falling gently down on the houses of the sleeping inhabitants. Even Pongwiffy is asleep. She is lying in a sea of mince-pie crumbs, dreaming of riding a red-spotted Pantomime Horse around a vast stage, with loud cheers ringing in her ears.

Beside her, on the pillow, Hugo is curled up in the

tea cosy he likes to use as a sleeping bag. At the end of the bed hang two stockings. One is the size of a postage stamp. The other is outsize and has a note pinned to it. The note reads: 'BROKUN LEG. GIVE JENERUSLY'.

Right now, both stockings are empty. But not for long. From far away, there comes the unmistakable silvery tinkle of bells. They are coming nearer . . .

Time to leave now.